A SAINT'S SALVATION

Beverly Ovalle

Mainstream Romance

Contemporary Romance

A Saint's Salvation

Copyright © 2016 Beverly Ovalle

E-book ISBN: 978-0-9967973-3-7

First E-book Publication: February 2014

Cover design by Dawné Dominique

Edited by M.S. Daniels 2016 and Magic Wand Editing 2014

All cover art and logo copyright © 2016 by Beverly Ovalle

PUBLISHER

Midwest Dragon Press

4
Beverly Ovalle

Dedication

I have to thank my son for his tattoo that gave inspiration to this story! Ooh Rah! I love you, my Marine, even when you drive me insane with your teasing!

Thank you to my editors (yes I had two! One for each edition) and I'd like to also thank the rest of the wonderful women who beta read and helped make this the story it became.

Thank you to all the men and women that have written that blank check for their lives to serve our country. They hand it over never knowing if it will be cashed in. I can't think of a braver or more wonderful thing to do. Please remember not all of the wounds of war are visible. It is not cowardly nor is it anything to be ashamed of if you reach out for help. Please do, casualties of war should be on the battlefield, not on the home front.

Don't know who to approach? Seek out your nearest Veterans Center whether you are active duty or a veteran. We never want to leave anyone behind.

Veteran's crisis hotline is 877-838-2838 (VET2VET) this is a confidential line.

Veterans Crisis Line is 1-800-273-8255 (VA Center) press 1 or text 838255 this is a confidential line.

I hope you all find your happy ending.

A SAINT'S SALVATION

Beverly Ovalle

Copyright © 2016

8
Beverly Ovalle

Chapter One

The need to be home was eating him up inside. He needed to walk down a street without Kevlar on and his rifle at the ready. He wanted to sleep knowing guards weren't necessary. He wanted to drive and not worry about IED's. He wanted a day where death threats weren't common place. He needed to be home. He needed to be with family, despite the heartache he faced.

Nick knew going home was going to be hard. After nearly four years of being away and the last seven months in Afghanistan, he felt the need to reconnect. The folks had been good about not nagging him to visit, but Nick knew they missed him.

His little sister, though, had been nothing but a pest. She was always asking when he would be back, but his sister was not little anymore and in the past year, she'd stopped asking.

Nick felt as if he was unraveling. He needed arms around him, someone to hold him. Nick wanted, needed to feel safe again, to feel hope again. He needed to know that what he had done had helped preserve the way of life back home. He needed the comfort of family and friendships untainted by war.

Nick lived the motto *Semper Fi*, always faithful. He maintained his unwavering faith in God. He was faithful to his family and friends. Nick was faithful to her, when it had mattered. Most importantly he was faithful to the Corps.

Nick received the Dear John letter a couple of months into his deployment. Worn out, tired and miserable in the conditions here, he'd looked forward to her letters. She was tired of a boyfriend on the other side of the world and wanted someone to go to the movies with, arms to hold her at night. She didn't want to hear of war and death. She wanted someone to lean on, someone there. Nick felt as if she had broken his soul.

His buddies called him Saint. Nick wasn't by any means. He swore and drank and smoked. The guys called him Saint because no matter what else he did, Nick was always faithful to *her*. Not that it mattered anymore. She had just been the final tear in the cloth of his soul. The emptiness inside him was frightening.

Leila had never been one to carry the light. The crevices of her mind were dark, her eyes holding an ancient, unhappy soul. They were drawn together like a moth to a flame. At times, she couldn't even bear to be around him, his joy more than she could sometimes stand. High school sweethearts, they epitomized the ideal that opposites attract.

Perhaps she had seen the darkness now inside him, the absence of the joy that drew her. The combination of him and her, looked at in that light, was frightening in the extreme. She must have dreaded it. For self-preservation, if nothing else, she had to let him go.

A shout from Hamilton brought him back to the here and now. "Hey, Saint, do you see any trouble coming?" On guard at the west wall, Nick shook his head. Not that it was much of a wall, a couple of sandbags holding up a makeshift bullet riddled wooden fence, an illusion of safety and security.

"No, it all looks clear." Well, as clear as normal, Nick thought. The Seabees and the Army Corp of Engineers had done their best to give them a clear line of site, but the rubble of buildings and piles of rock where there used to be a town never seemed to go away. Rebels constantly hid there, randomly firing at their FOB, a forward operating base in Helmand Provence, making it almost impossible to build a more secure perimeter.

Nick could see kids playing in the dirt. In the distance the locals were harvesting the poppy fields. Some of the largest poppy fields in the world were right outside the walls of the FOB. Beautiful when in bloom, they were more pervasive and did more damage than the terrorists.

"Any more threats?"

"When aren't there threats?" Every damn day there were threats. "Why, is there a problem?"

"The brass is making noise. When they do something stupid, we end up paying for it." Hamilton sounded disgusted. As he spoke, shots were fired over and through the fence, adding more holes to the dilapidated barrier. Nick and Hamilton hit the ground, rolling toward the sandbags to return fire through the cracks. "See what I mean?"

"Yeah, it's been a while since they shot at us, at least a couple of days." Nick's sarcasm caused Hamilton to laugh.

"Probably someone is coming to pick up something from the poppy fields and they want to keep us from seeing who." Hamilton glanced at him. "You doing okay?"

"Gettin' there. It was just a shock, ya know?"

"Yeah, damn women. The least they could do is be faithful while we're out here fighting."

"Yeah, it sucks. I just can't help thinking it's my fault."

"Fuck. How the hell could it be? You weren't even there. The bitch knew you were gone, were going to be gone." They fired shots, aiming at the muzzle flash in the distance. More Marines headed their way, sprinting from cover to cover. Perez came running, bringing out ammo and providing more fire power.

Another crack and Perez went down with a cry, dropping the ammo cans in his hands.

"Fuck! Medic! Man down!" The cry went out, passed through until the call went to the corpsman, while Nick pulled Perez under cover. Keeping low so he wasn't a target, Nick tried to stem the blood flowing from Perez's wound using the keffiyeh he wore to keep the dust out of his mouth. It was dusty and sweaty but easily available. Hands pushed his away. Nick looked up. Petty Officer Jones, better known as Doc, had bandages ready.

"Help me roll this on until we can get him out of here." Her voice sent a ripple through him. Nick had always ignored the attraction he felt for her. He had his girl back home, and fraternization out here could get him thrown in the brig. Not to mention the brig out here was a hell hole.

Nick was leery about approaching Doc now. The Dear John letter was a shock. Hell, he'd known Leila for years, friends since they were little. Her betrayal was unexpected. Nick didn't even really know Doc. He could trust her with his life, but he wasn't ready for another go around with his heart, no matter the attraction he felt.

Nick looked toward the fence line, rifle at the ready. Shots were firing sporadically around him. That's when he saw it, the trail from a grenade launcher, unmistakable. *Shit!*

"Cover! Grenade incoming!" Nick shoved Doc, sending her sprawling over Perez and covering the both of them with his body. There was no time to run. "Fuck!"

The grenade went off. His ears rang, masking the sounds of the fire fight.

The dust settled and he sat up. His stomach turned. Numb, he froze, staring at the woman beneath him. He tried to draw in a breath, but his lungs seized at what he saw. Nick would never forget the sight of all that blood. Her screams pierced his soul, tearing through the ringing in his ears.

"Doc!"

Her nails dug into his arm as his nickname whispered off her lips. It sent chills down his spine. She went boneless beneath him. Nick sucked in a breath, fearing the worst. He snapped into action grabbing Doc's radio. "Medic! Doc's down. Repeat, Jones is down."

He could see his buddies firing, the rat a tat tat he knew. The sight of muzzle fire, the jerk of M-4s and M239 machine guns as shots were fired and brass flew attested to their determination to bring the enemy down. Nick ignored the shots around him and assessed the situation. His brothers in arms would show no mercy with two of their own lying injured.

He quickly grabbed his kerchief and wrapped it around Doc's calf, swallowing hard. Her foot was shattered. Grabbing his KA-BAR, the handle of the knife sturdy enough for what he needed, Nick formed a tourniquet above where her ankle used to be, stopping the flow of blood. Nick twisted the KA-BAR until it stopped. His heart ached and he realized that feelings for the doc were there. Whether he wanted them to be or not.

Another corpsman arrived. The shooting had stopped. The man with the grenade launcher was lying in the dirt, not moving. *Good, the son of a bitch is dead*, Nick thought. Jones was carefully lifted onto the litter that had originally been intended for Perez. A second litter arrived for him. Nick watched them being loaded and then manned a litter to help carry them to the HELO deck. He didn't want to let Doc out of his sight until he was forced to. The senior corpsman, Dane, was calling for an emergency helicopter.

Nick set the litter down next to the landing area. Dane was shooting something into the doc and Perez. Nick's heart clenched as he took a last look at Jones before he turned to walk away.

"Hey, Saint, stop right there." Nick stopped and looked at Dane. "What the hell happened to your back?" Dane came over and put his hand on Nick's arm. Pain shot through him and the world went dark.

* * * *

Angel cursed the dust that seem to cover every inch of sick bay. She'd like one day where she didn't have to clean up just to get everything dirty again. She peeked into the waiting room. There was a line at sick bay, as usual. Minor injuries for the most part, the result of horseplay among men letting off steam, but occasionally they were more serious.

There were three corpsmen that served on this little out-of-the-way base in Helmand province. She was one of the few women on the base and the first one to arrive. When Angel finally convinced her parents that the Navy was her choice, placating them with the fact that she was going into the medical field, Angel never dreamed she'd end up in a combat zone.

She'd treated more shrapnel and gunshot wounds than she'd ever thought she would. She was proud to be one of the first women in combat, at least officially. There were reports of women dying in combat since Desert Storm. The American people turned a blind eye and ignored those deaths, pretending women hadn't been out in front for decades. To be one of the first officially assigned to a combat zone was an empty honor.

Angel sighed as she heard gunshots. Hopefully they would not result in any wounds. She or one of the other corpsman would be called if necessary. The Navy corpsman had little to do with the scuffles around the perimeter of the base other than patching up the Marines.

Angel looked around sick bay. It was as clean as it was going to get. It was time to start calling in the first of the injured. She checked the sign in sheet and glanced at the waiting room. She'd go in order unless there was blood.

"Private Schuster, follow me."

One Marine stood up and sheepishly followed her, limping as he walked. Great, she thought, this one was probably injured lifting weights. Rolling her eyes, she gestured towards the examining room. Hardheaded, every last Marine on the base had nothing better to do than lift weights and play pranks. This one had probably done both. Shaking her head, Angel headed into the room behind him.

She heard the radio crackle as she entered. It was never silent. Sick bay kept it going just in case they were needed. There wasn't always a Marine around to send to run to get a corpsman in case of a serious injury. The sound of gunshots echoed as a Marine screamed into the open channel.

"Fuck! Medic! Man down!"

Ignoring Schuster, Angel cursed and ran past the Marines in the waiting room, grabbing her bag as she headed out following the unnecessary directions where help was needed. She just followed the gunshots as she headed outside followed by the contents of sick bay as the Marine's in there shouldered their ever present rifles and followed. Injured or not, they didn't back down from a fight. Especially if one of their own was hurt. Angel knew there would be no mercy from them.

Breathing heavy and swearing she'd start working out more, Angel slid to the corner of a building nearest the fire fight. Enemy fire had the Marines pinned down and she could see one wounded Marine with another trying to stop the bleeding. The Marines that had followed her gestured, moving into position to lay cover fire so she could reach their fallen comrade.

Her blood thrummed, pounding in her ears as her eyes darted looking for the safest way to make her way forward. Taking a deep breath Angel darted, using what cover she could, zigzagging her way to the Marine that needed her.

Sliding in next to the wounded Marine she pushed her way in, her bag already open and ready. She shuddered as a zap of electricity raced from her hands to her heart.

"Help me roll this on until we can get him out of here."

Without looking she knew the Marine trying to staunch the blood. Santiago. Saint as he was known by his fellow Marines. Ignoring the pounding of her heart she got to work trying to save Perez as Santiago assisted as best he could.

"Cover! Grenade incoming!"

Angel didn't have time to respond before her breath was forced from her, flattened by Santiago who was heavier than she expected. God damned Santiago had shoved her forward onto Perez. She only hoped she hadn't hurt him worse and then her world exploded.

White-hot pain seared through her. Angel's heart seized, her breath caught in her lungs. A burning sensation tore across her body. She forgot about Perez and Santiago, her world narrowed to the screaming nerve endings in her body. Gulping in air, the high-pitched screaming stopped and she realized it was coming from her. Angel looked up into the regretful eyes of Santiago.

"Saint." The whisper escaped her lips. Overcome, the pain indescribable, Angel grasped his arm and darkness over took her.

Beverly Ovalle

Chapter Two

Nick woke up in the hospital. His first thought was of Doc, making him realize how far he had fallen without even knowing it. Buzzing a nurse, Nick inquired about her. He already knew she had lost her foot. His stomach turned remembering the carnage. He couldn't lose her; he'd just found her. Hopefully, his actions had saved her life. She could live without her foot. He wasn't sure he could live without her in his life.

Hearing that Petty Officer Jones was in surgery solidified his determination to see if his attraction was returned. Nick had never felt anything like the jolt he received when the doc touched him. Thinking that she died from the grenade woke him up to the fact that his hurt from the Dear John letter stemmed not from the loss of the girl he thought he loved, but from her betrayal of the ideal she represented. The ideal of home and family he hoped he could have with the doc.

Nick made sure his family knew nothing about his time in the hospital. He begged his superiors not to send notice home. His injuries were not life threatening, so they reluctantly agreed. If he hadn't worn his helmet and flak vest he might not have made it. The worst was how deeply the muscles in his butt had been cut from the shrapnel. Not something that he really wanted disseminated, especially among his raucous family. Nick shifted on his belly, his butt aching. No way did he want his family to know.

The hospital bed was not made for back wounds. Each and every time he rolled over in the middle of the night, white hot stabbing sensations woke him. He glared over at the chair in his room. More specifically, the donut sitting on the chair in his room. It was either stand or use it. The weakness in his legs made the decision for him each and every time.

Today was the first day he'd be able to leave his room. It had been all he could do to make it to the chair for a change of pace. Looking at the clock, Nick decided it was time to get up. He'd insisted. Doc couldn't come to him. So he would go to her. Reports weren't enough anymore. Nick had to see her for himself.

Inching closer to the edge of the bed, Nick hissed as he slowly twisted and swung his legs, one by one, off until his toes met the floor. His feet firm on the cold tiles, Nick took a deep breath and let it ease out as he pushed himself upward from the mattress. Stopping when his arms were fully extended, he stood, waiting for the throbbing in his wounds to ease.

He had thought pushups in boot were hard. Hell week was a cake walk. He knew that now. Gritting his teeth, Nick stood completely up. Gravity pulled at his stitches. He shuddered, barely breathing. The whisper of his hospital gown finally covering his pride and joy was ignored. Air still flowed around his exposed rear. At the moment, breathing against the agony was paramount.

"Pain is weakness leaving the body. Pain is weakness leaving the body." Nick whispered the words, hoping it would help. "Pain is weakness leaving the body." He sucked in a breath. "Fuck that."

Pain was pain. His drill instructor had no clue. Hissing Nick shifted. If he could stand for just a minute more. Nick watched the door. Soon. It cracked open followed by a nurse. Finally. He'd only seen this one a couple of times before. Nick wondered how many there were in the hospital.

"You're a stubborn one." The nurse wheeled in a chair. "Here you go."

Nick's eyes widened at the sight. He swayed.

"Hold on." The nurse bustled over. Carefully grabbing his arm. "Sit in the chair. It will help."

"Fuck no." It burst out of him. The thought of sitting had his body tensing. It set every stitch throbbing.

"Then back to bed."

"No. I want a walker." Nick shook his head, grimacing. "Well, I don't want one, but what else can I do. No way can I sit. No way."

The nurse flipped over his chart, read it and then glanced back at him.

"No wonder. All right, I'll bring in a walker." She wheeled out the chair. The door closing silently behind her.

Nick stood, once again trying to relax his muscles.

She was back again in a few minutes. This time she had a walker in front of her. By the looks of it, the Cadillac of versions.

"If you have to, use the seat. It's better to sit down in pain than fall down. Think of how that will hurt." She positioned it in front of him. "Leaning down will immobilize the wheels. That way you can stop if you need to."

"Thank you." It didn't seem like rocket science but he'd heed her words. He didn't want to fall. That would hurt and set him back. He needed to get back to his unit. Once he was sure Doc would be fine. "Please hand me my donut then." He pointed to the chair.

"You're prepared." Her smile changed her face. Lit up the room.

Nick couldn't help but smile back. "Of course I am. I'm a Marine."

She rolled her eyes. "Taking a stroll around the corridor? I'll follow if you'd like."

The draft as he leaned forward and grasped the handles reminded him of his state of undress. "I bet you'd like that. Your own peep show."

She laughed. "Oh yes, the look of raw meat excites me every time." She turned and opened the solitary cabinet in the room. She shook out a gown and came over. "Here you go. We can put this on like a robe. You'll be protected from any and all roving eyes."

Nick lifted one arm from the walker, extending it out for the nurse. Unless it was the doc admiring him, he'd prefer to be covered.

"You know that putting on the other side will hurt." She slid it up his arm, carefully settling it on his shoulder. "I'm sorry." She eased his other arm back, dressing him much like she would a baby.

Nick couldn't stop the exclamation of pain that escaped. The nurse tugged settling the gown across his shoulders. Nick straightened his arm, the most painful part done. He'd be damned if he took off the gown any time soon. It's not like he could shower yet any way.

He took the walker in hand and with determination, set out. He passed the nurse, holding the door open for him and turned left. He already knew where doc was. It was time to check in and see how she was doing.

* * * *

Angel gazed around. Everything was fuzzy. Her lips were numb, her leg ached. She didn't want to feel anything. She refused to look down. Her ears still rang from her own screams. She knew when the pain got to be too bad, she could press the button and feel the warmth flow through her veins. It was temporary at best and probably addicting.

She didn't think the doctors were worried about that at this point though. Angel didn't think she would either. She just knew if she looked down, if she peeled back the bandages, it would look as if her leg was hamburger meat. She didn't know how long she'd been out. Long enough to get to the hospital.

The last thing she remembered was hearing the whirling of the helicopter blades. Even that was overshadowed by the remembrance of the hot, itchy, burning sensation. Her breath caught. Nothing could describe it. Thinking about it sent tremors through her body and sweat beading down her forehead.

Angel didn't want to look down and see the reality. She knew that her short career was over. The Navy had no need for a one legged corpsman. The fact that some officer thought it necessary to tell her that she'd be getting a Purple Heart as she was getting ready to go into surgery seemed surreal. Like that would make up for what she'd lost.

Her eyes itched and the bridge of her nose got tight. Wet warmth trailed down the sides of her face and pooled against the collar of her hospital robe. She knew she was in pain, or she would be if she wasn't so drugged up. She moved her tongue searching for any moisture. Her mouth tasted as if she had eaten an ace bandage.

Probing at her lips with her tongue she felt them peel away from each other, as dry as the inside of her mouth.

"Here, take a sip of water."

Angel swore it was Saint talking to her. She was too lethargic to try to move her head to look. A straw was slipped between her lips. Angel sucked and cool moisture flooded her mouth. Greedily she swallowed more. Releasing the straw, she lay back against her pillow. The tightness in her head and ears a reminder not to move.

"I'm glad you're alive. I thought for sure you weren't going to make it."

Angel sighed. She wasn't so sure she was going to make it. She wasn't sure how she felt about being alive. Despair welled up in her. Her gut twisted while the throbbing in her sinuses had her head aching. Minor compared to the pain radiating from her leg, but Angel was sure that losing her foot couldn't possibly be the only injury she had.

She knew from her studies what a grenade blast would do. Ringing in her ears, missing body parts, cuts from shrapnel all were common. It hadn't prepared her for the reality. The constant pain and despair. How she wanted to scream at the world. It wasn't fair.

Why, she wondered, did the grenade not kill her outright?

"Doc, Doc?"

Angel could hear the scrape of the legs of a chair on the floor. It sounded like Saint, but there was no way it could be. Even if it was, she didn't want him to see her like this. She breathed deep, a sob catching in her throat. She would never have a chance with him now.

"Jeez, I'm an idiot. You're in pain and I'm here pestering you." Angel heard a sigh and soft lips heated her forehead with the moisture of a light kiss. "I'll see you later, my Angel."

Her eyes closed, Angel listened as the soft *slap slap* of slippers shuffled across the floor. The whisper of the door being pushed open and the *woosh* as it closed let her know her visitor had left. The fluorescent lights emitted an ever present buzz, insinuating even into her dreams. She drifted off to sleep.

Waking, Angel wondered who had been with her. Doped up and in pain she decided she would worry about who it was another time. Her world was out of whack. She didn't know how much time had passed. Light and dark and pain jumbled together. Voices and smells assaulted her senses whirling together in a blur.

"Doc?"

She knew that voice. It had been there every time she woke up. It had to be a dream. The throbbing in her leg told her it wasn't.

"Saint?"

"So you do know me." He sounded relieved.

Angel had to wonder why.

"How long have I been here?" She frowned, eyes still closed to keep the spinning at bay. "Why are you here?"

"It's been a couple of weeks. Once I could leave my room I came to visit you every day."

"Why are you here?"

"In the hospital?"

Angel slowly nodded her head. The dizziness was beginning to pass. Snippets of Saint's visits passed through her mind. Here she thought it had been wishful thinking.

"Yes."

"The grenade was a bitch. It decided to share the wealth."

Angel opened her eyes, the room steadying. Saint was looking at her, a crooked grin on his face.

"How bad were you hurt?" He was on top of her when it exploded. How was he standing in front of her? He seemed virtually unhurt.

"I'm healing. Lucky for me, I had my flak vest on. It took the brunt of the shrapnel." Nick sighed. "That was too close for comfort Doc. I don't know how the three of us survived. One of God's miracles, maybe."

"Perez is okay then?" Angel yawned.

"Other than the bullet hole, he is."

Angel nodded and yawned again, her eyes fluttering closed against her will.

"I'll be back later, Doc." She felt lips against her forehead and sleep claimed her.

* * * *

Angel cracked her eyes and moved her head toward the window. Her curtains were cracked enough to see a man outlined, looking out the window. She must have made a sound to capture his attention.

He turned and walked slowly toward her. Saint. She hadn't been dreaming him.

"How are you feeling?"

Angel realized he was using a walker. Ignoring his question, she had one of her own.

"What's wrong?" Her arm pointed toward it.

"Nothing time won't fix." Nick shook his head. "It just gives me something to lean on if my legs get wobbly."

Angel grunted. Since she hadn't made him up, he'd obviously been up and moving longer than her.

"How's your head, Doc?"

"Clear. Why?"

"Just wondering. You've been in and out of it for the last couple of weeks."

"Hmm." Angel had no idea of what to say. She wanted to wallow in her despair. Mourn the loss of her foot. Cry to the heavens and ask why she lived. She couldn't do that though. Not with Saint here recovering from wounds he'd gotten while saving her.

Angel had never seen him look so serious. His eyes were sad when they looked at her. She didn't want his pity. Her hope for something more fizzled. Angel didn't even realize she'd still hoped. She thought losing her foot would have put the kibosh on that.

"Feel up to a game of cards?" Saint made his way to her bedside table. "If there are any in here."

"Sure." Angel wanted the company. What she didn't want was to be alone with her thoughts.

"Got some." Saint flashed the cards and a grin. "How about strip poker?"

Angel snorted. "Right. I don't think so."

"Fiiiine. You chose."

"How about Crazy Eights?"

Saint rolled his eyes. "How about War?"

Angel turned her face toward the ceiling, willing the sting in her eyes away. "I think I've had enough of that."

Saint stilled. "Crazy Eights it is." Saint pulled over her table and positioned it so they could both reach. It was a bit awkward but it worked. He pushed his walked against the bed and gingerly sat with a grimace.

"I'll deal."

Angel nodded. Just the small interaction was making her tired. She watched Saint deal and admired the strength of his fingers. They fell into an easy camaraderie, laughing and playing until Angel yawned, her eyes drooping.

"I'll let you rest." Saint gathered up the cards. "I'll see you later." He leaned over and kissed her forehead. A brotherly kiss except for the shock that travelled through her body at his touch.

Angel nodded, slipping into a deep sleep, too tired to worry about it.

She woke, disoriented. Rubbing her eyes, Angel yawned and stretched. The curtains were closed and faint light seeped in around them. It could be dawn or dusk, she wasn't sure which. The hospital seemed quiet, so she couldn't tell. There was no clock that she could see. Her bed had been lowered so she'd managed to sleep through the nurse checking in on her.

Angel wondered if she'd see Saint again. The thought of him had her heart racing.

"Shit." She had to stop that. He pitied her, nothing more.

"Morning." Saint popped his head in the door.

That answered the question of the time of day. Angel hit her remote button to raise her bed up a bit.

"I must have slept through the night."

He eased in the door, looking behind him and closing it quickly.

"Must be nice. Every time I roll over I wake up."

"Why?"

Saint turned and pulled up his hospital attire, flashing his muscular butt at her. "These."

Angel bit her lip, trying to stifle her gasp. She just wanted to grab on and squeeze him.

He dropped his gown and turned around. "I know. I have to look a mess. Frankenstein's monster butt. I'm going to look like I had a cheese grater to my ass when the scars heal."

Angel snorted. She hadn't noticed the stitching, too busy ogling his bare behind.

"It's not so bad. I could barely even tell."

"I can. It hurts to sit too long." He grabbed something off of his handle and flashed it. "That's why I have this."

Angel looked closer. It was a blow up donut. "I thought those were for hemorrhoids."

"Is that a polite saying I'm a pain in the ass?"

His grin had her laughing.

The door opened.

"There you are. You need to get back to your room."

The nurse shooed out Saint, shaking her head with a grin on her face.

"I'll be back."

Angel laughed at his poor Terminator impression. Shaking her head, she raised her bed up a bit more.

"That one's a pest." The nurse nodded toward the door. "Always asking for updates on you."

Angel smiled, happiness tapping at the edges of her heart. "He saved my life."

The nurse stopped and looked toward the closed door before swinging back around.

"Hmm. I never would have guessed. I suppose that's why." She came over and began fussing with the sheets. "Tomorrow I want to change your sheets. We'll get you in the shower and I'll do it then."

Angel wrinkled her nose. She was starting to smell. Sponge baths could only do so much. The thought of a shower was appealing.

"That sounds nice."

The nurse refreshed her water and checked her IV, changing it out. She changed the catheter bag attached to the bed.

"If I can have a shower, can I get rid of that?"

"Is it bothering you?"

"Yes."

"I'll talk to the doctor. Now time for sleep. You need to keep healing."

She checked the time and added another bag to the IV. Angel knew that whatever she added would knock her out, but also dull her pain. The routine was getting familiar.

Angel dozed and woke a few times throughout the day. Saint's face made an appearance at least once. Angel didn't know if it was a dream or he if he really was there, sitting next to her bed.

Morning sun once again woke Angel. There was no doubt it was day. The sun shone brightly, dust motes dancing in the rays streaming across her room.

No Saint. A thread of disappointment crossed her mind. Angel blinked, trying to clear her head and wake up a bit more.

"Good. You're awake. I chased out your shadow. Time for that shower we were talking about."

The nurse lowered the head of her bed. Angel yawned. Warm from sleep, she wasn't sure how she felt about getting wet.

"I've some help."

The nurse and a corpsman carefully scooped her up and placed her in a wheelchair. The IV bag and line were attached to a pole on the wheelchair. So much for hoping that the needles would be taken out.

Angel shivered. The plastic seat and back were chilly. They had managed to set her down without catching her hospital gown. What she wouldn't give for her footie pajamas. Her comfortable go to when she was ill. Angel sighed. They would no longer work. She didn't have two feet to put into them.

The nurse wheeled her into the shower area. It was large enough for the wheelchair. Angel swallowed her disappointment. She'd hoped that maybe she'd be able to stand. She knew that was an impossible thought.

"Time to strip."

The corpsman disconnected her IV from a plastic connector taped to the inside of her elbow. The nurse whisked off her gown and started the water. Angel started when a few drops of cold water splashed her. The water gradually warmed up, steam billowing from the shower head. The nurse turned the faucet adjusting the temperature.

"Let me know if it's too cold or hot."

Angel leaned her head back, the warmth spreading with each bead of water sliding down her skin. The wet warmth pooled beneath her buttocks, relaxing her further. She felt boneless.

"Like that?"

"It does feel good."

"You'll enjoy me washing your hair then."

"Mmm. Yes, please."

Angel didn't think she could stand another day of greasy stringy hair. The water tugging at her ends and the massage of the nurse's fingers in her hair and against her scalp had her eyes drooping. Idly she wondered how she could still be tired.

The liquid heat pounding against her shoulders and running down her body erased all embarrassment of having to be bathed. Angel leaned forward letting the spray and the bubbles rinse down her back. She moaned and managed a small smile at the nurse's chuckle.

"I thought you'd enjoy this. The first full shower after surgery is better than anything in the world."

Angel nodded. She didn't have the energy to reply and she wanted the shower to last as long as it could. She relaxed and let the water wash away the pain in her soul. For the moment all she felt was peace.

The water started getting cooler. It was time to go back to reality.

"I'm done now."

The nurse turned off the shower spray. A couple of chill drops chased down her spine dribbling from the end of the shower head. Angel shivered. A metallic click indicated the hose was once again stashed away. Angel could hear the nurse moving around the bathroom. Her footsteps returned bringing her closer.

"Lean back and I'll get your hair dry."

Angel did and sighed as the rough towel began blotting her hair, stroking it until most of the moisture was gone.

"Now leaned forward." The nurse dropped a towel around her shoulders wrapping Angel's hair in another. She pulled her wheelchair back and came around to finish drying Angel off. "Now let's get you dressed again."

Angel wrinkled her nose. She saw another hospital gown coming her way. What she wouldn't give for a pair of her nice comfy silky pajamas. There was absolutely nothing soft about the gowns. The corpsman came in at a signal from the nurse.

"Hold your arms against your body."

Angel held them tight and wrapped her arms about her waist. The corpsman grabbed her by the elbows embracing her against her own body and pulled her up slightly from the wheelchair. The nurse quickly slid a towel under her absorbing the water on the seat and drying her bottom off.

Angel could feel her face burn. More than anything that brought the helplessness of her situation to the forefront of her mind. She was eased back down, her hospital gown tucked beneath her, giving her the illusion of protection. Thin as it was, it was better than the sense of vulnerability she had while being manhandled, no matter how gently, after her shower.

She sighed and sat back against the wheelchair. Angel took a deep breath and another.

"Are you ready to return to your room?"

Angel nodded. Feeling refreshed and clean she only wanted to get back to her bed. Let the blankets cover up her legs so she could ignore her stump. It didn't seem quite as real then.

The two were easily able to maneuver her back to bed. The scent of freshly dried sheets wafted to her nose. Her door creaked open. She turned her head to see Saint stick his head in the door with a smile.

"All done?" Saint slipped in her room.

He looked her up and down. His eyes heated.

Angel had to be mistaken. He couldn't be attracted to her.

The nurse settled the last of the blankets over her lap shaking her head with a smile. "You're turning into a real pest."

With a dramatic gasp and hand over his heart Saints eyes widened. "Who, me?" He flashed a grin, and wielding his walker, came over and settled in the chair at the side of her bed.

Angel tried to stifle giggle at his antics. Saint stayed for a while entertaining her. Her eyes began to droop and he disappeared.

It began to be a daily habit. One Angel knew she shouldn't get used to.

Waking once again, Angel sucked in a deep breath. A sharp pain cramped her leg. She gasped. Some days the pain was worse than others. It eased only to start throbbing so intensely it took her breath away. Tremors plagued her legs and arms. Convulsively, she grasped the cylinder in her palm and pressed down on the button that would spread relief through her body. The pain occasionally flared up after a round of desensitization. Necessary, the doctor told her, in preparation for her prosthetic.

The heat spreading through her veins had her limbs loosening, her hands relaxing. Angel sighed. She focused on the relief, the world around her fading away until she heard voices outside her door.

"How is she?"

Angel wondered the same thing. *How am I?* The first few days after surgery had her welling in a vast pit of despair during the times she was cognizant. She wouldn't talk to the doctors or the shrink they sent her way, only Saint. He teased her, kept reality away. The weeks following as she healed were an emotional roller coaster.

Bitterness filled her mouth, the sour taste churning her stomach. She knew she was at her darkest upon waking up. The dreams of destruction and pain and of what might have been kept her sleep restless. Saint and his cheerful outlook couldn't help but improve it.

Angel knew who asked the question. Saint. Only he would dare.

Angel wanted more than friendship but she could see the guilt in his eyes as he looked at her. His constant flirting hid it but she knew the guilt was there. The sorrow on his face when he thought she wasn't looking at him. Like he should have saved all of her when if it hadn't been for him, she would have died.

His constant presence at her bedside was torture, but a pleasant one. Saint made her forget. She craved his company for that reason alone. Knowing better than to take his flirting seriously, Angel held him at arm's length. She knew she needed to protect her heart. The heart that already felt like it belonged to him. The more she got to know him, the harder it became to know he wouldn't be there with her forever. He deserved better, a whole woman, something she no longer was.

Turning her head just the tiniest bit no longer set off the beat of drums in her head. It gave her a chance to look at him. She bit back a giggle and sobered. Angel couldn't believe she found something to laugh at. Yet how could she not?

His back to her, standing in her open door was Saint. His Cammie blouse over his hospital gown. A snicker escaped. His open hospital gown, showcasing the angry red scars on his muscular butt. He had no shame.

Dammit, how can I laugh?

"Well? Is she doing better?"

"The petty officer is doing as well as can be expected."

That was a non-answer if she'd ever heard one.

"When will she be released?"

"She has a long road to recovery. First her limb has to continue healing. Then she'll be outfitted with a prosthetic leg. Then lots of physical therapy."

"But she'll get better?"

Angel heard a sigh and echoed it. That was the million-dollar question.

"She should. She's doing as well as can be expected."

The heels of the doctor's shoes echoed as he walked off down the hall. Angel stifled the urge to cry. Her emotions had been up-and-down since she had woken up in the middle of the night, seesawing from highs to lows. She blamed most of it on her medications.

Angel wouldn't even consider the fact that Saint would soon be gone. His healing wounds, the ones he was baring to the world, showed proof of that. He brought joy into the room with him. His smile and a teasing glimmer in his eye making the day more bearable

"You awake?"

Angel startled, opening her eyes. She hadn't realized she'd closed them again. Saint was looming over her with a grin on his face.

"Yes."

"They still won't give me my clothes. You're a corpsman. What's up with that? Look at what I'm reduced to wearing." He spun giving her a view of flying hospital gown, his Cammie blouse and bare buttocks.

Angel giggled.

"I don't see anything wrong with it."

"Right." Saint flopped down into the chair next to her bed, then grimaced. "My butt is going to freeze off."

"Don't be so melodramatic. You know your wounds need to heal properly."

"I think everyone just likes to see my butt." He grinned at her. "It is mighty fine."

Angel rolled her eyes. "It's just a butt."

Saint jumped up and turned toward her, whisking his gown away, and waggled his ass at her. Angel stifled a laugh. No way would she let him know how much she liked the view.

"Come on, this is one fine specimen."

"Like I said, it's just a butt."

Saint looked at her over his shoulder, a wide grin on his face. He touched his ass and shook his finger, blowing on it.

"It's sizzling, Doc." Saint winked and sat back down. "And, it's almost healed."

Angel's smile died. That meant he would be leaving soon. She understood that. The day he'd staggered into her room without his walker, grabbing at the walls to keep upright she knew. She didn't want him to go, but she didn't want him to stay. Her emotions were a mess.

She glanced down at her leg. All she could see was bandages. She could even wiggle her toes, all ten of them. Despite the fact that her foot was gone. When she shifted or tried to move, the pain began and reality set in.

"So, how about a game of Acey Ducey?" He was pulling over her hospital tray table as he reached down for his backgammon game. Saint was always ready to entertain her. He seemed to spend his every waking moment in her room. It was probably guilt. Angel could see it in his eyes when he thought she wasn't looking at him.

Angel focused back on Saint. "Sure, why not?" She might as well enjoy his company while they were together.

After that? She would learn to live with her disability. Or not. Angel didn't see much to look forward to. She had a daily visit from a shrink here and he was referring her to a psychiatrist back in San Diego. Evidently her attitude wasn't what it should be. Imagine that.

Chapter Three

Nick's family didn't know he was coming home. He hadn't been sure when he'd be able to get leave or how long he would have, so he decided to surprise them. He'd been back in Okinawa for a couple of weeks, back from the hospital for almost six months. Each day without a word from Doc seemed longer than the last. He finally gave up writing. She wasn't going to respond. He couldn't help getting depressed. His natural exuberance turning into gloom.

His Staff Sergeant recommended the leave. It was approved immediately upon his request, to his relief. But with Christmas around the corner, getting a flight home could be a problem.

Luckily, he'd been able to catch a military hop to Los Angeles. He had a two-day layover in LA and then a flight brought him in on the twenty-second to Chicago. Nick had a special layover planned there, so he wouldn't get home until Christmas Eve. He wanted to surprise Mom and Dad and knew there was no better date than that.

Nick had to fill the aching hole eating away at him. He needed to know he counted and not just for his service. That he was a man, a brother, a cousin, a son, someone valued for who he was, not just for being a Marine.

The grenade attack had been a beginning. It made him realize that his heart was bruised, but not broken. Nick still needed something, *someone* to hold him, someone to make him feel alive again. It made him realize that his life was not over. It gave him hope for a future. What was meant to be an ending, instead gave him hope of climbing out of the darkness that surrounded him. Hope that a wounded angel had given to him.

Nick needed his family, he knew this, but he also needed more. He needed Jones, but it wasn't meant to be. Nick needed to be wanted, needed the passion brought back into his life. The shrink he'd seen during his recuperation and had talked to for the duration of his deployment had suggested a way. Nick smiled in anticipation. It was something he never imagined himself doing, but his shrink assured him the Military Assistance Dating Website was legit. The man even had a hand in running it. MADWebs was something the guys joked about.

Hell, Nick had rejected the idea until he talked to a couple of his buddies. Turns out a couple of them used MADWebs and they were in some of the healthiest relationships Nick had seen. That's what he wanted. Reassured it wasn't a place for military groupies to spin their webs, Nick asked for his shrink's assistance. He happily gave it and helped Nick set up his blind date. Nick needed to feel wanted, even if it was just for a night and it seemed tailor made for that and more.

Nick had finished booking his flights. He extended his layover in Chicago and made arrangements to stay at the W Chicago Hotel along Lakeshore Drive. His mom would be so jealous. She loved that part of Chicago and often expressed her wish to stay there.

But first, he had two days in L.A. Nick pulled out his phone as he exited the plane. He found the number he wanted and dialed. It rang a couple of times before it was answered.

"Yo! Who's this?"

"Nice way of answering your phone Primo! It's Nick."

"Hey Primo! Watcha doin'? It's great to hear from you. La familia is glad you made it safe out of Afghanistan. Are you home?"

"Sort of. I'm at LAX." A smile broke out on his face. "I'm here for a couple of days and need a ride. Think you could come get me?"

"Shit!" In the background Nick could hear Alejandro telling someone where he was. Nick could hear excited screeching. "I'll head right over, should be there in less than an hour. What airlines, coz?"

"American, international arrivals. Gramma got room?" Nick was laughing. "Do you think she'll mind?"

"Shit, no! Don't you hear her in the background?" Alejandro laughed. "Tio Mateo is coming too." Nick could hear talking, doors shutting and an engine roar. "We're on our way."

"Awesome! I have to head to customs. I should be done by the time you get here."

"Cool. We'll see you in a bit."

They both hung up, excited to get together. Nick and Alejandro had been closer than two peas in a pod growing up, according to their moms. Born five months apart, they were more similar than different. Even when Nick's parents had moved to the Midwest, they'd stayed close. Hell, they were each other's wing man. One would chat up the girls, while the other got the numbers. No one could resist their charm when they got together. Jandro and Nick had sworn to go into service together, but when Nick went, Jandro stayed behind to help his mom, Nick's Tia.

Nick could feel the hole inside him closing. Family was his saving grace. It had been almost four years since

Nick saw la familia. Almost all of them had come to his boot camp graduation in San Diego. The family in L.A. had driven down. His parents and sister had flown out. Grandma and Grandpa had driven their RV out from the Midwest. The whole family had converged on the base to see him graduate. It was the last time Nick had seen them all at once.

An irrepressible grin split his face. Having taken a military hop, Nick was in dress blues and looking a little rumpled from the long flight. On his way to customs many people stopped him to shake his hand and give him a hug, people he didn't even know, and emotions swelled in his chest.

Marine directives dictated that they not wear their uniform when flying for their own safety, but it was required on the hops. Nick hadn't flown in uniform before. Tired as he was, Nick stood even prouder. Now Nick understood the phrase barked at him throughout boot camp, Stand Proud! Nick had always thought it should be stand tall, but the emotions inside him made him realize that he was proud, and so were the people around him.

Nick needed this, the connection to his country, their pride in him, just for being a Marine.

When he got to customs, Nick was shuffled to the front. Busy as it was, as much of a hurry as everyone was in traveling this close to Christmas, it touched him. Marines don't cry, but with the generosity of the people around him, he felt his heart swell. He was passed forward one handshake and hug at a time. At the head of the line, the last person to let him through was a lady that reminded him of his mom.

The lady gave him a hug, one that was tighter than most. "Thank you and God bless you." Nick hugged her back and as he let go, Nick noticed a pin on her coat. Nick gave her another hug, a longer one. She was a gold star mom. She, more than most, knew the sacrifice asked for by our country.

"I'm sorry for your loss."

She gave him a sad smile. Nick could see tears in the back of her eyes. "Semper Fi, Corporal. Now get going.

I'm sure your family is waiting for you." Nick smiled at her as she nudged him to the customs desk. Nick realized that it could have been his mom wearing the pin if God and luck had not been on his side.

"Semper Fi, ma'am." Nick placed his bag on the desk and opened it, pulling out his ID. The customs clerk checked it and waved him through.

"Welcome home, Marine."

Nick turned back to face the crowd and gave a salute to them all. "Merry Christmas." Nick grabbed his bag and headed out to a chorus of good wishes and applause. The hole inside was slowly closing. Coming home had been the right decision.

"Primo!" Nick looked up and laughed. Alejandro and his cousins were there to greet him. Nick was embraced by them all at once.

"Let me breathe!" Nick laughed. "I lived through Afghanistan and you're going to smother me in L.A. Nice!" Nick hugged them all back. "Where's Tio?"

"He's at the curb. Let's go get your luggage." Jacinta had him by the arm, tugging him toward baggage claim.

"I didn't bring anything other than my carry on. So, we can go."

"K." Jacinta smiled brilliantly up at him.

"Good thinking." A short shove by Alejandro had them all laughing like loons.

They headed out the door to pile into the waiting SUV. Nick crawled in the back seat and leaned over to give Tio Mateo a hug. "Hi, Tio! Thanks for coming to get me."

"No problem, mijo! Everyone wanted to come, but these three beat them to the car." Mateo turned to maneuver the car into traffic. "Glad to be back in the U S of A?"

"Yup. I need to be back at the airport in two days. Can you take me?"

"Not staying for Christmas? Abuela will be disappointed."

"It was the only flight I could get home. Hey, don't anybody tell my mom and dad I'm here. They don't know I'm coming home for Christmas. I'll arrive on Christmas Eve. I want to surprise them."

"How are you getting home from the airport? Isn't it like two hours away?" Alejandro had visited during high school and had remarked on the long stretch of fields between towns. The drive seemed to go on forever to him.

"Mmm hmm. I have arrangements made to pick me up. All I have to do is call and let them know when I'm arriving."

"They are going to be so excited." Jacinta chimed in.

"When was the last time you saw them, Mijo?" Tio Mateo asked.

"Almost four years now since I've seen them. Dad picked me up from South Carolina when I finished training and took me home for a week before I left for Okinawa."

Jacinta gave him a hug. "I'm so glad you came to see us. Mama Rosa is thrilled. She can't wait to see you."

"The girls are heading over." Lee added. He had been texting continually since they hopped in the car. Nick enjoyed being here, his cousins were all within a few years of age as him and they loved to get together. Their parents would always exile all of them to the yard while they stayed inside and gabbed.

"I wasn't sure I'd be able to see you all. I came in on a military hop from Japan. This was as far as it could take me. When I checked for flights home there weren't any for two days. So, I'm on the first one I could get out and that left me time to visit here. I hope I can see everyone."

Alejandro had been on the phone and hung up laughing. "Well, primo, the whole familia is heading over, looks like we'll need to get out the barbeque." Nick could see the grin on his uncle's face in the mirror. His family was always ready for a fiesta. "You're the family's VIP today."

The happiness that showed in their eyes due to his presence, began to weave through his soul.

The drive passed with talk about what had been going on over the last few years. When they pulled into the yard, it was packed with la familia. It looked like everyone had been able to get there. Nick supposed that flying in on a Saturday morning had worked out well. A few were still at work, but all his primos and primas were there. Nick got out of Mateo's truck and headed straight to his grandma.

"Gramma!" Nick gave her a big hug, lifting her off of her feet. Not too hard to do since his grandma stood about four foot nothing!

"Mijo!" She laughed. "I'm so happy." Grandma was beaming. He could see she was happy to have him home. Nick put her down on her feet and started the round of hugs. This was just what he needed!

* * * *

She hated being home. Thank God she was able to stay on base, even if it was in the hospital. Each visit with her parents left her drained. This morning was no exception. A bouquet of flowers preceded her father into her room. They were obviously from the church garden. Her mother had her hands full of envelopes.

Dammit, more get well cards. Angel knew they were sincere wishes but what good did they do? They couldn't help. The sympathy cards were the worst. She hadn't died and how could they know what she was going through? Her mother placed them on the table next to her bed.

"You can open them later if you like."

Angel didn't even bother to answer. She just gave a sharp nod, not that her mother saw it.

Her father nodded and sat down. Her mother hovered behind him, looking everywhere but at Angel. One glimpse at her leg was all it took for the tears to start.

Her mother went into hysterics every time she looked at her leg, or what was left of it, and today was no exception. As if she didn't feel bad enough. Her father praying over her made her heart ache. He'd started almost immediately after he sat down.

She couldn't stand it anymore. She had to stop him. The worthless prayers rubbed her nerves raw.

"Where was God when I was hurt?"

The pain in his eyes when she questioned him let her know that her doubt in his faith was painful.

"You survived."

"Big, fat deal."

It wasn't the answer that Angel wanted. She wanted to go back in time. She wanted her leg back, not the plastic hunk they were fitting her for. She wanted a redo. She knew she wasn't going to get it.

Her mother cried into her handkerchief. Who used those anymore? Her mother, of course, the fifties throwback of the perfect wife and mother. The white cloth hung limply from her hands, wet and mascara stained as she wept into it. She hadn't even seen her siblings, her mother wouldn't let them come. She was afraid of upsetting them.

Her father shook his head and prayed some more.

Angel gritted her teeth and tried to ignore them. The churning in her stomach was almost more than she could bear. The tic of the blood rushing through her temple set her head throbbing.

They finally left her in peace, leaving behind the get well wishes from her father's church.

Angel knew praying was her father's answer. He was the minister of a small church. She had grown up running around the church. She looked around her room at the get well cards sent by the congregation. She'd known her father's parishioners all her life. A large extended family related by beliefs.

Her lips tightened and she swept the cards to the floor. It wasn't like she could grow her leg back. No amount of sympathy and well wishes would make it better.

She had been transferred to San Diego shortly after Saint left. Angel picked at the covers over her legs. He had written to her and Angel read the letters and carefully saved them. She wouldn't write him back, though. No matter how much she wanted to. She didn't want his pity. She didn't need his guilt. What she wanted was something she could never have, especially now.

Saint had spent part of each day making her laugh. He had made her forget while he was there for his own recovery. She could almost forget she wasn't whole. Her laughter stopped when he was sent back to combat. For a while she hoped that the two of them could have something more. Reality set in when he had gone back to his unit. Her days were quiet and filled with pain, treatments, and medications that had her floating. The time dragged by.

Coming home made something inside her shrivel up. Saint wrote to her weekly, for a while. Angel didn't know what to say. She was depressed and bitter. Angel knew it would show if she wrote to him. He had continued to write longer than she thought he would with no response from her. His last letter came months ago.

He had gotten her through the first couple of months. It wasn't right to expect him to get her through the rest of it. If it hadn't been for his heroic actions she would be dead. Even if some days she wished she were. She hated the physical therapy. She hated the fake foot. She hated the constant reminder that her life was no longer the same.

Staring at the floor and the cards scattered there, Angel watched them blur. A warm trickle down her cheeks had her sucking in a breath. She wouldn't cry. Her father was right. She'd survived. It was up to her to live.

Rubbing her eyes, Angel turned off the light. Her feelings for Saint had deepened day by day. She wouldn't ever see him again. Angel doubted she'd be allowed to stay in the Navy. Not with part of her leg gone. Especially if her emotions didn't steady. There was no place for her to ever even run into him. She was born and bred in San Diego and he lived somewhere in the Midwest.

Heart aching and tears still escaping only to dry and tighten the skin on her cheeks, Angel pulled up the covers, and turned to her side. Her gut was knotted from the anxiety of the last few months. She was mentally exhausted. She decided that it was time she turned her thoughts to something positive. Something she could do. Getting better and seeing what lay in store for her. Maybe her dad was right. Maybe God had a plan for her.

Tomorrow she'd see the shrink, or at least make that appointment they'd been badgering her about. She'd even give that stupid hunk of plastic a chance. She wasn't the only serviceman to be injured. It was time to stop feeling sorry for herself and begin to live again.

Her life had changed and it was time for her to embrace that. What she'd hoped for, worked for and dreamed of was in ashes. She was determined to rise again, to become a phoenix in her own life. Angel snorted. She was getting poetic. That so wasn't her. Whatever, she was determined to change. She was sick of wallowing in self-pity.

Angel reached over and turned off the light. Pulling the covers over her head, she curled into her pillow and closed her eyes.

Tomorrow. She'd worry about it all tomorrow.

Beverly Ovalle

Chapter Four

What had started out as a family get together had turned into a work party. Showing off and trying to one up each other had led to working on his Tio's house next door. Tio was expanding the house to accommodate his growing family. Nick enjoyed the work. It helped him feel like part of a larger whole.

Nick, Jandro, and Lee had a competition going to see who could finish first. Thanks to the three of them, the frame of the second floor was completed. Tio Mateo had started the wiring and cable that he planned to run through the upstairs and another uncle had started on the plumbing. Some of Tio's friends were coming to do the roof after Christmas.

The goofing around, watching the little ones, helping Grandma, all gave him a sense of family again. The Corps gave the same, but this was blood, La Familia.

Nick was grateful no one had commented on his scars. Working bare-chested and in shorts, the whole family had seen them. Shiny as new scars were, they still told a story Nick didn't want to talk about. Nick had scars on his neck, arms and legs. The lightest scaring was on his back where his Kevlar had kept him alive. Grandma and the women in the family had all patted him and gave him hugs and kisses. The men had slapped him on the back and hugged him tight.

Late that night Nick sat on the roof with Jandro and Lee, laid back, shirtless, sweaty, and dirty. Admiring the work they had done next door. Grandma came out and scolded them, but had gone back in smiling and shaking her head.

"Primo." Jandro looked at Nick as he cracked open a can from the six pack at his side. "I see you have some pretty fancy medals."

Nick just nodded. Lee sat back, drinking and grinning.

"I'm still handsomer than you, Primo." Jandro grinned. "The medals and those little nicks won't help you one little bit with the ladies."

Nick choked and laughed, spraying Jandro with beer.

Jandro jumped up, wiping his chest off with a discarded shirt.

"Hey, that's my shirt!" Nick laughed.

"Yeah, to wipe off your spit, primo! What a waste of a good beer!"

Lee laughed at their antics. Lee was the quiet one in a family of extroverts.

"I'll have you know, the ladies love me. Now they know how brave I am, you'll be looking at the dregs, my man!" Nick smirked at Jandro.

"Pussy. These handsome features trump those itty bitty scratches any day!" Jandro laughed then sobered. "Primo, glad you are okay." Lee nodded in agreement and just that easily, it was done, another bit of darkness banished and the band around his heart lightened some more.

Nick couldn't believe how fast the time went. The two days flew by. Connecting again with his family was great. Grandma was getting older. Nick hadn't realized how much, until he saw her again. But, with so much of the family around, his grandma was well taken care of. Quite a few of them still lived there to take care of her.

Each hug helped, showing Nick that he mattered, showing him that he was loved. It was hard leaving, but Nick was looking forward to seeing his mom, dad, and sister. Even better, Nick was hopeful that he would be billeted in Oceanside or San Diego. Nick kept that to himself, knowing nothing was sure until his orders were cut.

Nick was advancing to sergeant when he got back to Okinawa. The date was already set. He had been in Oki for almost four years, having extended his tour there. His home base, it was also the central operations for Operation Enduring Freedom and deployment activities in the Pacific

Rim. His time in Okinawa had been spent going back and forth from Afghanistan, Korea, and the Philippines. Nick had been back from his deployment for debriefing and reintegration when he left to come home for a visit. It had been the first time he had asked for combat leave and it was approved, helped along, no doubt, by his psychiatrist and his Staff Sergeant.

Being stationed in southern California close to his familia would be great. It was only a two-hour drive, max. Nick could visit, especially on those long ninety-sixes. As long as he didn't pull duty, Nick could be with family for holidays. It would be a win-win situation all around!

Nick gave everyone a round of hugs. Grandma was teary eyed, but knew Nick had to go.

"Gramma, love you." Nick gave her a long hug. "I'll try to visit more often, 'kay?"

"It's okay, Mijo. Keep safe." Nick finally let her go, standing still as she blessed him, something she had done his whole life. Everybody gave him a second hug and kisses and then they were off. Grandma's head bowed, still praying as they drove away. Tio Mateo was driving again, while Alejandro rode shotgun.

"Tio, are you the official airport driver?" Nick joked.

"Sure seems like it. No one else wants to fight the traffic. Since I worked near the airport for so long, I guess it just makes sense. I know the roads here better than anyone." Mateo grinned at Nick. "We're going to miss you. You stay safe, okay? Are you going back to Afghanistan anytime soon?"

"No, after a couple of tours I didn't volunteer again. I'm due for new orders soon though. Not sure if I'll get what I requested, so I'm just waiting."

"Well, make sure we have your address, Mijo. And call once in a while, or Skype. I'm down with that, you know?"

Nick laughed. "Sure, Tio. I get it." Alejandro just snickered.

"Gonna miss you, primo." Alejandro added. "It's been fun. You ought to think about getting stationed here."

"Jandro, the closest would be Pendleton. Or there's always Twenty-nine Palms."

"Nuttin' in L.A., huh?"

"The closest is the Hollywood Marines." Nick laughed. "That's what the boots are called that go to Pendleton."

"Shaaa. Wat's up with dat?"

"Who knows? Probably the boots from Parris Island are jealous, 'cause we're all so good looking!" They both laughed.

The ride to the airport went quickly, surprisingly when it was so congested, but that was L.A.

"Tio, thanks for leaving so early. I hope I don't get grounded! I think the weather is good back home though. I hope it stays that way." Nick was peering out the window. "Man, I'm going to miss the warm weather here."

"Do you have a direct flight there?" Mateo asked as he maneuvered up to the curb at departures to park.

"No." Nick shook his head answering as they hopped out of the SUV. "I have a layover in Chicago. That airport is a madhouse normally. I don't know what it will look like on Christmas."

Nick gave Tio Mateo and Alejandro hugs. "Thanks, guys. I really needed to see la familia. The last year has been really hard." Nick smiled. "Coming back helps me see why I do what I do. Love you guys!"

Another round of hugs and then Nick turned to enter the airport. Jandro stopped him with a hand to his arm and then flung it around Nick's neck in a headlock, Jandro's typical wresting move.

"Primo." Jandro looked him in the eye, loosening his arm. "Remember we were going to go in together?" Nick nodded. "Shit, man, if we had gone in together…"

"No." Nick shook his head. "We might not have even been stationed together. We're the two eldest males in the family. We would never have been stationed together, let alone deployed." Nick grabbed Jandro's arm. "I'm glad you weren't there. It was bad enough. If something had happened to you. Shit!" Nick shoved Jandro back. "Look at this, trying to make me into a weeping pussy!"

Both laughed. "Primo. Glad to see you're still a jerk." Jandro was grinning at him. "Man, I wanted to let you know. I signed." Jandro looked at Nick. "I signed, primo. I head to boot camp in January. Shit. You're the only one who knows."

"Tia is going to kick your ass." Jandro nodded in agreement.

"I know, but it is something I have to do. You know that. We should have been doing this together. I just have to catch your ass."

"Crap." Nick flung his arm around Jandro. "Shit. Damn it, man! Be safe. And don't be no pussy in boot. I did it and I know you can too." Nick glared at him, his chest tight with pride. "Stay safe, primo. I expect to be seeing my wingman in one piece."

"Who's the wingman?" Jandro cocked a brow at Nick. "Ah, go primo. You don't want to be late."

Jandro laughed and with a final hug they stepped back and grinned at each other. Nick turned and headed in, glancing back over his shoulder. Tio Mateo and Alejandro were waving as Nick entered the terminal doors.

"Yo, Marine, Ooh Rah!"

Nick saluted, waved and went inside. He already had his ticket and boarding pass. He headed straight to the security line after checking his gate on the monitor. Luckily, military members had head of the line privileges. They had a special line along with premier flight passengers. It made it so much easier. The security line was huge!

Nick headed to the military line and gave his pass and ID to the TSA agent. Nick then dropped his bag on the conveyor and took out his laptop. Next were his shoes and coat and garment bag with his blues. Now he was set. Nick moved forward at the agents signal and entered the body scanner. A quick slide in and out and Nick exited to grab his gear. Nick was always tempted to give them a little waggle in the scanner to see what they would do, but restrained himself. Grinning, thinking about their reaction, he quickly put on his shoes and coat. After putting his stuff back in his carry on and grabbing his garment bag, Nick headed to the gate.

He sat down in one of the remaining seats. The airport was packed with holiday travelers. His flight didn't take off for another hour, but the loading should be getting ready to start soon.

Nick looked around. The coming holiday had imbued the crowd of people with cheer. A hum of excited conversation was buzzing around him. Nick smiled. The merriment seeped into his soul taking another sliver of his emptiness away.

The two days, though not long enough, had once again kindled the flame inside him. Nick had hope, and the sense of connection that had been slowly lost over the last few years. The sense of connection that he'd thought had been broken inside him with his last deployment. With that sense of hope and joy, Nick looked forward, even more, to his next adventure.

The air hostess started loading the plane. Nick checked his ticket. He had a while to go. They were loading first class and those needing assistance first. Huh, Nick looked up, surprised. They were also loading active duty military. Nick sauntered up to the gate and handed over his boarding pass and showed his ID.

"Merry Christmas and welcome aboard. Thank you for your service." The hostess smiled as she scanned his ticket and ushered him through.

Nick checked his seating assignment and headed into the plane to locate his seat. From those already on board the plane and the people still waiting to board, it looked like the flight was almost completely full. It made him glad he had been able to get a flight home for the holidays. Nick asked the flight attendant if there was room in the hanging closet for his garment bag.

"I'm sorry, sir. Those are for first class passengers only."

"Okay. Thought I'd ask." Nick shrugged.

"Can I ask, is it a suit for Christmas?"

"No. It's my dress blues. I didn't want to have to press them again."

A man in one of the first class seats spoke up. "I think being a Marine is first class enough. Why don't you go ahead and hang them. Is there room?" The last part was directed to the flight attendant.

She opened the door to check. "Yes, sir, there is." The attendant turned to Nick. "Here, you can give them to me and I'll put them in for you."

"Thank you, ma'am." Nick nodded toward the man. "Thank you too, sir. Merry Christmas."

"You're welcome, son. Thank you."

"Don't forget to retrieve them when the flight is over," added the attendant.

"I won't." Nick checked his ticket and headed toward his seat. It was good he was over the wing. His mom swore those were the best seats. Nick was especially glad he had an aisle seat, as cramped and crowded as it was, he would need the room to stretch out. Nick double checked his seat to make sure he had the correct one. He did. An older lady occupied the window seat. She looked like she was ready to fall asleep. The middle seat was empty so Nick figured he would have to get up again.

Nick looked around watching people get settled. It was almost time for takeoff. People were chattering and settling down, rear ends sticking into the aisle as they settled their bags under the seats.

The flight attendant came through, checking seats and closing overhead doors for those bins that were full. She passed and Nick glanced up. Coming down the aisle was a familiar face. One Nick never thought he'd see again. Nick couldn't stop the smile that spread over his face. He gave an appreciative whistle. Eyes snapped to his, narrowing until they saw him.

Nick watched a smile spread across her face. He stood up and went to meet her. Wrapping his arms around her, crutches and all, Nick kissed the top of her head as he gently hugged her. His body stood at attention, electricity racing through him at the feel of her body against his. He didn't want to let go. Nick knew better than to take it further though. Doc had never given any indication that she felt the chemistry he did, treating all his advances like he was joking.

"Doc, whatcha doing here?" Nick asked as he released her.

"Catching a plane, Corporal, what does it look like?"

"Are you traveling by yourself?"

Her eyes narrowed, a frown forming over her face. "I'm a big girl. I can travel by myself." Doc sniffed. "Are you traveling by yourself?"

Nick laughed. "Of course. I'm a big boy." He leaned closer and whispered in her ear. "Wanna find out how big?" Nick waggled his eyebrows at her.

Doc laughed and pushed him away.

"Down you Devil Dog. I didn't put up with your shit there and I won't here either."

"Where's your seat?"

"Here, on the emergency exit. I'm not sure they'll let me stay there due to these stupid crutches."

"Just sit. They'll let you know." Nick grabbed the bag Doc was trailing behind her. "Here, let me put this up." He swung it up in the overhead, pushing bags around until it fit while she sat down.

"Thanks. Where are you heading?" Doc settled back in her seat, putting her crutches next to her with a sigh.

"I'm heading home for Christmas. Wisconsin. What about you?" Nick moved to get out of the aisle. He was in the row behind her. He stood, leaning over her seat to continue their conversation. Nick blinked, his attention captured as he looked down. Doc was wearing a very pretty, low cut sweater. From this angle he had a perfect view of her red lacy bra and the curvy flesh it hugged. Nick reached down and quickly adjusted himself. He'd been at attention since he hugged her.

"I needed a break. I'm visiting Chicago, heading to see a VA doctor there about a new prosthetic, before I go back home."

"Home being where?"

"San Diego." Doc looked up at him and glared when she saw where his gaze was. "What do you think you are doing?" She snapped her fingers in front of his nose, breaking his line of sight. Nick grinned unabashedly at her.

"Admiring the view."

"Sit down," she said and he chuckled. Nick swore Doc was grinding her teeth, probably trying not to punch him. He seemed to have that effect on her. Whereas Doc was the reason Nick started to realize his heart wasn't broken. Not to mention other parts south. Nick supposed it was no wonder she never responded back to him. He seemed to frustrate her to no end most of the time and it wasn't even on purpose.

"Okay, Doc, don't get your panties in a twist." Her long drawn out sigh sent joy pinging through him. He knew he was perverse. "I'll behave." Her muttering made it seem like she doubted his sincerity, and Nick admitted that Doc might be correct. He couldn't seem to stay away from her and all she did was push him away. "I swear."

Doc looked at him. "Then sit down. They won't let you stand the whole flight anyway." Her statement was born out when the flight attendant approached.

"Sir, you need to sit down and fasten your seat belt."

"Yes, ma'am." Nick winked at her as he sat. She shook her head with a smile and walked away. He could hear more muttering from the doc. Nick snickered quietly. He didn't need to aggravate her more than he had. "Truce, Doc?" Nick peeked at her through the seat crack.

She looked over at him and gave a short nod. "Truce, Corporal. It's a long flight."

They both settled back. There were just a few more passengers boarding. One was a harried mother with a small child. She was checking tickets and talking agitatedly with the flight attendant. They both approached, checking seat assignments. They stopped as they got to his seat.

"Sir, would you mind exchanging seats? The lady here couldn't get seats together with her child and would prefer to sit with him."

"The center seat is one of yours?"

She nodded. "My son's. I'd really rather sit with him, but I couldn't get seats together."

"No problem, I'm traveling alone. What seat do you have?" Nick looked at her ticket.

"The window seat there." She indicated the one in the aisle in front of him. Nick's heart beat harder in anticipation, right next to Doc. Perfect.

"Not a problem at all." Nick stood up and edged out of the seat. "Here you go. Would you like me to put your bag up?" She smiled at him a little wearily.

"Thank you." Nick tossed her bag up in the last open space above. He stepped back to let them get seated. Nick couldn't move into his seat until they were settled.

"Thank you, the airline would like to offer you a complementary drink for your assistance. Just ask when the beverage cart comes through." The stewardess smiled at him.

Nick winked. "That would be awesome, though it was not a problem at all. Really."

"I'm sure." The attendant acknowledged. "Please settle in as soon as you are able."

Nick nodded and edged sideways as she scooted past him. The aisle was so narrow she brushed against him regardless, leaving a pleasantly soft imprint on him as she did. Nick looked over. Doc was rolling her eyes at him.

"What?" Nick wagged his brows at Doc as she shook her head and laughed.

"Where are you sitting now?" Doc looked at him and grimaced. "Can you help me get my bag when we land?" Nick could tell she hated asking for help.

"Of course, Doc." Nick and stepped over her legs carefully. "I'm your new seatmate." He sat and leaned close. "It was me or the kid."

"Really?" Doc raised her brow. "I'm not sure I wouldn't have preferred the kid."

"You wound me, Doc." Nick placed a hand over his heart and rubbed. "I can feel it bleed."

She sniggered. "I'll warn you now. I'm beat and plan on sleeping once we get in the air." Doc looked down and sighed. "I had physical therapy this morning before I left. It kinda takes a lot out of me."

"I know it does. I'll even let you use me as a pillow."

Doc shook her head at him, obviously grasping for patience.

"All right, all right. You know I'm just teasing you."

"I know." Doc sighed. "It's just been hard. Highs to lows. I'm not on an even keel yet and I'm tired."

"I wouldn't mind being your pillow." He muttered under his breath. Nick leaned over and gave her a hug. "I'm here anytime you need to talk. You know that, don't you?"

Doc nodded and smiled.

Nick could see the weariness and the pain seeping into her eyes. "Go to sleep, Doc. I'll wake you when we land."

Nick sat back and sighed. He wanted the woman beside him. She might look as soft and delicate as a flower, but Doc was tough as nails. She was a pint size piece of dynamite. Doc responded better to aggravation than sympathy. Nick had found that out at the hospital. Teasing her had helped him, it gave him hope that he hadn't strayed too far from the man he used to be. God, his family would love her. She'd fit right in with the jibes and trash talk with his Primos and his mom would love that Doc didn't take his shit.

Nick hadn't seen Doc since he left the hospital, not until she walked down the aisle of the plane. It had been months. She stirred up feelings that he wished he could take to fruition. Nick sighed. He sure hoped that MADWebs had found him a match, though Nick was doubtful as he was pretty sure his match was the curvy little corpsman sitting next to him.

Nick looked at her as the plane took off. Doc really must have been tired. Before the plane was horizontal, she was asleep. When she started to whimper in her sleep, Nick lifted up the arm between them and undid her seat belt. Nick pulled her into his arms, resting her head on his broad chest and she settled down, the obvious nightmare going away.

He tightened his arms around her and laid his head on hers. Nick could get used to this and if Doc had been reliving the same nightmare he always had, Nick was glad to have helped. His eyes slowly closed as he settled into sleep.

The pilot announced that the plane was getting ready to descend. Nick couldn't believe the flight was almost over.

He yawned, waking up. Nick looked at the bundle in his arms.

"Doc," Nick whispered. "Time to wake up." She groaned and snuggled deeper in his arms. Nick laughed. Doc would not be happy if she was awake. "Reveille, reveille all hands on deck." Her head bobbed up, her eyes blinking. It was guaranteed to wake a sailor up. No matter how deep their sleep, reveille seemed to be every seaman's built in alarm clock. "We're getting ready to land, Doc."

Doc shook her head and looked around. Pushing away from his arms, she glanced at him. "I must have been out like a light." Doc shivered and smiled. "I guess you meant it when you said you'd be my pillow." She stretched. "Damn, it's cold."

"We are landing in Chicago, you know. It is winter." Nick buckled his seat belt. "Put your belt on Doc, time to go down." A light blush coated her cheeks as she slid a glance at him from the corner of her eye. His eyes gleamed. "Doc, are you having dirty thoughts? Naughty, naughty!" Doc got even redder and glared at him. "I'm just teasing." Nick leaned over and kissed her cheek. "But if you're interested..." Nick smiled at her, mischief all over his face.

"God, you drive me bonkers. You know that, don't you? How the hell did you ever get the nickname Saint?"

Nick laughed.

"Maybe one day I'll tell you." Nick waggled his brows at her. Her sharp bark of laughter made him grin.

They landed and waited to disembark. Doc preferred to wait until most of the people were out of the way before she exited the plane.

"You can go on, you know. I'm perfectly fine."

"I know. I'm in no hurry. Do you have a ride?" She nodded. "Do you have your cell phone, Doc?"

"Yes. Why?" Doc flashed him a pouch hooked on her crutches.

"Handy. Here, give it to me." Nick grabbed her phone and started punching in numbers. His rang and he grinned.

"Now I'll call you back, so you have mine." Doc shook her head and rolled her eyes. It rang and Nick saved it to contacts, then fiddled with it some more and handed it back to her.

"What exactly did you do to my phone?"

"You'll see." Nick gave her a quick kiss on the head as they stood up, turning to retrieve their bags from the overhead compartments before she could voice her objection.

They slowly descended the ramp into the terminal. Nick had remembered to grab his garment bag before they exited the plane. They stayed together until they passed the security check point into the main airport. A Navy corpsman hurried over to the doc.

"Petty Officer Jones? I'm your ride to the VA Center." He glanced at Nick. "Is he with you?"

"No. He's a friend I met again on the plane. He's just giving me a hand." Doc turned to Nick. "Corporal," she cleared her throat, "Thank you. Have a Merry Christmas."

Nick pulled her into his arms and gave her a hug. Doc hugged him back, holding tightly to him. If Nick didn't know better, he'd swear she didn't want to let go.

"You have a Merry Christmas too. Remember to call me if you need anything. Even better, if you want anything." Nick kissed her head and reluctantly let her go. He handed her suitcase handle to her escort. "Here's her bag."

Nick turned to Doc. "I'm here until Christmas Eve." Nick swallowed and looked at her. "You are more than welcome to share Christmas with me and my family. My mom would have no problem with one more person."

"Thanks, but I'm not sure that I'll be free." Doc smiled at him and turned to follow her ride.

Nick still was still unable to determine was how she felt about him. She seemed to enjoy his company, but subtlety rebuffed his attempts to take their flirtations to a deeper level. Leaving him confused, yet hopeful. Meeting her on the plane had stirred all the feelings he had tried to suppress.

Nick watched her walk away. She didn't glance back, all her concentration on keeping upright on the slippery floor of the airport. Nick couldn't let her go like that. He pulled out his phone and dialed. He could hear her laughter as her phone started singing "I'm Bringing Sexy Back." She ignored it and smiled back at him. Nick thought, *that's more like it.*

Nick turned and saw a man patiently waiting, wearing the clothes that identified him as a W Chicago employee.

"I'm Nicholas Santiago. I take it you're my ride?"

* * * *

Angel walked away, not looking back at Saint. Once again her smile was lost. Her heart was aching, beating for the man she was leaving behind. Her phone went off. *Sexy Back* began playing and she snorted with laughter. Ignoring her phone, she turned to smile back at Saint. His grin told her all she needed to know.

Shaking her head, a reluctant smile in place, Angel turned back to follow her guide, ignoring the blaring of the song. Saint wasn't bringing sexy back, he had it in spades and always would.

Angel was finally taking steps to claim her independence and to bring her self-confidence back. She'd let her shrink talk her into trying to get over Santiago and who does she run into? Him.

Waking up with his warmth and heat next to her on the plane was a delicious dream, one she didn't want to leave. Normally she couldn't sleep without having a nightmare. Saint had kept them away. She knew because despite the time that had passed, she had them every night without fail. It had felt natural to sleep with his arms securely wrapped around her even if she didn't know how she had gotten there. Arms that kept her feeling safe and secure and made her world feel right.

He teased her like he had in the hospital, riling her up just to give her that shit eating grin. A tremor ran down her spine and her nipples in her lacy red bra tightened. Angel needed to forget all that. His flirting meant nothing, even if it felt like it did. She was on a mission, all part of the plan to prove she was still a woman, despite her handicap.

Her crutch slipped and Angel scrambled to keep her balance. She had to pay attention and concentrate. She had to stop thinking about Saint. The floors of O'Hare Airport were glossed to a high sheen, making it almost impossible to stay upright while daydreaming. The tan tiles with their black flecks reflected her own image back at her. How it kept its shine with the thousands of people that daily crossed them was a mystery.

It was a far cry from the ragged carpet found at LAX. O'Hare screamed money and sophistication. The shops were all high end. The artwork displayed above was centered in the corridors for viewing pleasure. Angel snorted. Who the hell would come here just to gaze at the art? Maybe it was there for those people whose planes were late, or maybe those picking them up.

The corpsman in front of her was moving a bit faster than she was able to follow. Angel figured at some point he'd realize that he was outpacing her. She wasn't about to go faster and end up in an ignoble heap on the floor. If Saint was still watching her, and she thought he was, she didn't want his last memory of her to be a pathetic amputee that couldn't even walk. She put a little extra swing in her walk, a smile lurking at the edge of her lips.

Angel felt the loss of Saint's eyes on her, the heat no longer keeping her warm. She shivered, the chill in the air seeping through her bones. December in Chicago? She must have been nuts to come here now.

The corpsman waited patiently at the doors.

"Do you need to collect your luggage?"

"Yes, thank you."

He gestured toward a large monitor listing flights.

"Your luggage should be on carousel three. It's just down the escalator here."

Angel stepped forward and gingerly stepped on the moving staircase. She wobbled and the corpsman quickly grabbed her arm to steady her as he moved behind her.

"Careful. No need to take a tumble."

Angel sighed. It was instances like these that brought home her disability. She wondered how her upcoming date would react. If she couldn't stand by herself, how was she supposed to convince anyone else that she was okay?

She shook her head and stood taller. Dammit, she couldn't go back down that road.

"Thank you. Sometimes I'm a little unsteady on my feet." Angel flashed a grin back at the corpsman.

"No problem. I'm from a small town and I had a hard time getting used to escalators." He chuckled. "I tripped down them the first time I rode one. I'm Petty Officer Nguyen. Peter."

"Petty Officer Jones, but you know that." Angel laughed. "Angel, or Doc as the guys in my unit called me. But I guess everyone where we're going goes by that."

"Pretty much." His deep laugh rang out. "We generally stick to last names or rank and name here." Peter grabbed her elbow as they came to the bottom of the flight. "Three is over here. Point out your bag and I'll get it." He steered her toward a row of chairs.

Angel rolled her eyes but followed anyway. "It's a seabag. I imagine it will stand out from the rest of the luggage."

"I'm sure it will." Peter set down her carryon and headed toward the carousel. "Take a seat, I'll be back as soon as I have your bag."

She settled down on the black vinyl and chrome chairs. Angel carefully arranged her legs to prevent anyone from running into her and leaned her crutches up against the arm of her chair. No luggage had been dropped yet so she figured it would be a while.

One bag came out, then two. Then the carousel was full and Angel spied her avocado green bag. Peter leaned over and grabbed it, checked the stenciled name and maneuvered back through the gathered crowd to her side.

"Got it."

"So I see." Angel grabbed her crutches and struggled to stand. "Thanks."

"No problem. We'll head to the base and I'll get you settled in the barracks."

"I'm not staying at the base, until after Christmas. I made reservations at the W on Lakeshore."

"Are you meeting family there?"

"My family's in San Diego. I'm meeting someone there, though."

Peter laughed and wagged his brows. "I get it. I'll drive you to the hotel. I can make arrangements to pick you up on the twenty sixth and take you to base. Will that work?"

Angel laughed. "I do need to check in today at the base before I go to my hotel. I've an appointment to pick up my new prosthetic. On the twenty sixth I've another appointment with more follow up. It won't be a problem shuttling me back and forth?"

"Not at all. I'm on duty again that morning." Peter nodded toward the elevator. "Let's get this show on the road."

Angel resettled her crutches under her arms. She might have been able to do without them, but she didn't have the confidence to do so on such slippery floors. She'd learned to anticipate needing them. Angel hoped that the new prosthetic she was there for would be better. She'd gone through a couple of legs since she'd gotten home.

Once she decided that she would get better, Angel had thrown herself into the therapy. With nothing else to do but get better, Angel had also started using the workout room at the hospital.

The self-pity and depression she'd wallowed in for so long had turned her muscles to fat. Angel had taken a good look at herself in the mirror and was appalled. She knew realistically that she couldn't have stopped what happened to her body. Unable to even walk, drugged out and in pain no matter what, Angel had been unable to do even the least of exercises.

Once she realized she wanted to live, that her life wasn't over, Angel was determined to take her life back. She'd gotten back in shape. It was a lot harder than she'd thought to get there. Maintaining her body took more energy than it ever had before. She knew it was because everything was accompanied by pain.

It was hard not to get depressed by her circumstances. If she dwelled on how her life had changed, she would cry. She'd done enough of it. She was looking forward, not back. Seeing Santiago was harder than she'd imagined. It didn't change her plans. Angel needed to get over him. Her plans for tonight would help. If she could go through with it.

Chapter Five

Nick stretched. He'd arrived with a few hours to spare before he was supposed to meet his date for the evening. After such a long flight, Nick needed to move around, so he headed to the gym. It was state of the art, a far cry from the piece-meal gym equipment that the Marines had cobbled together in Afghanistan.

Nick was pumped from his work out, but now he stunk. Normal after such a workout, but thankfully he was stateside now, not in the desert where the water was rationed. There was no way Nick wasn't showering before his upcoming evening. Even if he was spending the night alone, the hot shower was a luxury he wouldn't pass up after the poor facilities in Afghanistan.

Nick headed in to shower. Stepping into the steaming water, he started to relax. Soaping up was done with efficiency, habit from the five minute showers anyone with the Department of the Navy had to take by necessity. Nick laughed as he rinsed. He really didn't have to rush. He had time. Standing under the hot water, enjoying the warmth, he thought about the evening ahead and how he'd come to this point.

He was looking forward to it. Upon checking into the hotel Nick was told that everything was on the house, a tribute to his service. Arriving in his room, a message, along with a complementary bottle of champagne from his shrink greeted him. An anticipatory grin split his face as he read it. His date's name was Angelina. The suite was luxurious, a fitting place for seduction.

Nick turned off the shower, his fingers pruney, and got out. He peered in the mirror, wiping a small section away and grimaced at his reflection. He needed to shave. Nick grabbed his kit, looked into it and froze. The scent wafting out of his kit brought back small memories, the sound of gunfire, always when least expected, the quiet of the streets before a bomb blast, the screams of the wounded. Nick hadn't bothered shaving at Grandma's house, and he had evidently grabbed his combat shaving kit without realizing it. He shook his head, shaking off the feelings that wanted to creep out. Shaking the kit over the trash, careful to keep his gear from falling out, he let the sand and dust fall, throwing away the bad memories with the sand. He could do this.

It took strength to admit your weaknesses. Doc's courage made him reach for the help he needed, in spite of his reluctance in the beginning. Help that showed him how to conquer unexpected reminders like this.

Shaking his head, Nick gritted his teeth. Enough. Doc would never be his. Thinking about her would only taint his upcoming date. He took a deep breath and concentrated. Pushing away the sounds of battle that lingered in his mind, letting the memories go. Breathing in and out, Nick continued until his body relaxed and his hands stopped shaking.

Enough. He had new memories to make.

Straightening up, Nick finished his grooming. He wrapped the towel around his waist and headed to his closet to decide on a suit. It was easy enough, he'd only brought two sets of dress clothes. The hotel had pressed them for him while he'd been at the gym.

Checking the time, he noted there was still an hour before the date was supposed to start, no need to get all dressed up yet. Nick turned on the television, surfing channels to find something that caught his interest. *Rudolph* was on. Nick laughed. He felt a little like Rudolph, not quite fitted into the slot where he knew he belonged. Hopefully, like the red-nosed reindeer, he would find his perfect spot in the world. Donning his pants, Nick settled down to watch one of his favorite Christmas shows when his phone rang.

"'Lo."

"Hey, primo, you get in okay? Grandma wanted to make sure."

"Yeah, I did. I ran into a friend on the plane and I forgot about calling. Sorry."

"No problem. Hey, how you doing?"

"I'm good." Nick shrugged. He was too antsy to sit on the phone for long.

"Good, good. Look I got to go." Nick could hear Grandma in the background yelling. Lee was catching hell for something. "Shit. Mama Rosa's gonna get him with the broom!" Nick could hear the laughter in Jandro's voice. "I got to go, primo, before she gets me too in the fallout!"

"Wait, wait! What did Lee do?"

"Gramma found out he snuck a girl in last night. Oh, he's estupido that brother of mine!"

Nick started laughing. "Oh, he's in trouble."

"Yup. Gotta go!" Nick heard the phone hang up on Jandro's laughter. He hadn't had time to see if Jandro had broken his news about joining the Corps.

Nick shook his head, laughing. It was always the quiet ones! Nick was glad Grandma knew nothing of his layover. She'd probably take the broom after him too. The joy and laughter his family brought was immeasurable.

Dusk would be settling in soon. Nick looked forward to seeing what he hoped would be a spectacular sunset. He finished getting dressed, and checked his watch again, his heart beating faster when he saw the time. Not long now.

The instructions left little effort on his part. Drinks, dinner, and even dessert were arranged. Introductions along with drinks were to be in the romantic setting of the private balcony that his suite shared with the suite to his right. Dinner would be downstairs in the hotel restaurant, and then back to the balcony for a dessert bar. The balcony heaters were arranged to keep the temperature warm despite the below zero chill of December in Chicago.

The only information Nick had about his date was that her name was Angelina. Nick laughed at the irony, he would have an angel, one way or another.

A knock from the hallway had him opening the door to room service. Grinning in anticipation he watched as the waiter wheeled in the cart. The portable drink and dessert bar was supposed to be brought up when his date arrived.

Nick sat on the couch, staying out of the way as the waiter arranged the place settings and an ice bucket on the balcony table. The waiter pulled out the bottle of champagne, popped the cork, and poured two glasses. He set the first glass down and turned, handing the second glass to someone Nick couldn't see. She was here. His heart sped up in excitement.

The waiter set the champagne bottle back in the ice bucket and Nick stood up, his breath hitching. The waiter nodded and turned. Entering the room, the server dimmed the lights and pressed a remote lying on the table top. The Christmas tree in the corner lit up, the lights twinkling merrily and the low murmur of Christmas Carols coming from hidden speakers. Then the waiter quietly left and shut the door. Nick went over and locked it. He didn't plan on any interruptions.

Nick made his way to the glass doors. Exiting his room, Nick saw the outline of a woman. The sun was dropping, highlighting her, leaving him unable to see her features, only her shape. Nick sucked in a breath and could feel himself harden. Curvy and just the right height to fold into his arms, long hair that lay in waves down her back, she was perfect.

Nick could hear her suck in a breath, in surprise or appreciation? Nick hoped to find out. He moved closer and with the sun no longer in his eyes, surprise slammed him upside the head. Nick stepped forward, trapping her against the railing. Her face had lit up, her smile diamond bright. His soul burst with happiness, responding to the joy in her face.

"Hello, beautiful." Nick leaned down, pulling her curves against him and ravaged her mouth, not about to give her a chance to reject him. He felt her breath catch and then her arms came around his neck. He heard her glass hit the balcony floor. Nick shifted, sliding his lips along her neck. "I never dreamed it would be you."

****

Angel walked out on the balcony, cold and scared, ready to turn around and head back into her room. The ache in her belly telling her that she was making the wrong decision. Her heart cried for the man she'd walked away from at the airport.

Ignoring both, Angel wanted to feel like a woman again, even if it was with a stranger. There was no agreement the night would end in sex. It was a blind date to see if they were compatible. Angel had slid on her silky red dress, shivering as it slid down her body. The built in bra ensured she'd have some support but the sexy thong she had showed in the lines of the dress. Angel left it off, her stomach twisting at the lack of protection.

Angel had made her way out to the balcony and grabbed a glass of champagne from the waiter to calm her nerves. Taking a deep breath, she asked him to let her date know she was there. She downed the whole glass, trying to calm her nerves. Angel grabbed the bottle and quickly poured a second glass before the waiter even left the balcony. She needed liquid courage before she fell apart.

Glass in one hand and the other pressed to her stomach, Angel paced. She kept on her side of the balcony so her date couldn't see her.

It was not a mistake. It was not a mistake. If she repeated it enough, maybe she would believe it. She turned to face to where the waiter exited, keeping an eye on where her date should appear. She backed away, heading toward her suite. Her stomach churned. She couldn't do this.

If she made it to the safety of her room before he came out, she would stay there. This was a stupid idea. Angel knew who she wanted. It wasn't a nameless, faceless stranger. It was the man she'd left. Saint. When her date came out, she'd tell him this was a mistake. Maybe he wouldn't show. Angel wondered if that would be worse. If she stayed, and he got cold feet.

Saint was still in Chicago. He had to be. He'd been exiting the airport, not going to a different terminal for a connecting flight. She could call him, she had his number. Maybe he'd give her a chance. She could feel her heart thudding in her chest. She should turn around. Run before her date arrived.

Angel slowed, maybe Saint was being picked up. Wisconsin wasn't that far from Chicago. He could be gone already. Or maybe he was renting a car. She'd never know unless she called. Ready to turn around and abandon her date, she froze when she heard the slide of the glass door of the suite beside hers open.

A man stepped out. He raised a hand, blocking out the setting sun. Looking toward her. Angel's heart stopped, her breath caught in her throat. Moisture gathered at the juncture of her thighs while goosebumps covered her body. Never had she thought that it would be him.

Her smile had spread across her face while her heart sang. She was glad she hadn't cancelled. He stepped forward and Angel knew she'd made the right decision by the joy that spread across his face as he looked at her. There was no mistaking the emotions that crossed his face. Angel couldn't doubt any more that they were meant to be together. She would stop pushing him away.

She stepped toward him as he swooped, gathering her in his arms and kissed her. Angel's pulse raced and her soul rose to touch his. Every nerve in her body tingled. The beat of her blood blocked any sounds out. Her body cried for his, the rest of the world falling away.

The fierceness of his grip as he held her to him caught her breath in her throat. Sparks from his hands warmed her body. Angel had never, ever expected to be meeting Saint. The fact that it was him and she was in his arms was more than she could ever have hoped for.

His hard body against hers felt right. She snaked her arms around his neck and melted against him. She was tired of fighting her feelings, denying what she wanted. His lips, soft and firm against hers drew a moan from her.

Saint's hands slid down her curves. Angel shivered, gooseflesh breaking out all over. She pressed against him. She was done pulling away from him.

She was his.

* * * *

Nick ran his hands down her back. The thin silk dress she wore left little hidden from his hands. Nick smoothed his hands across her ass and pulled her up and fitted her heat against his growing erection. Nick couldn't feel any panty lines. With her arms around his neck, holding tight as he kissed her, Nick grabbed her thighs and wrapped them around his hips.

He slipped his hands under the short skirt of her dress, caressing the globes of her ass. He slid his hands inwards, finding as he hoped, no panties. Running his fingers lightly against her silkiness, and dipping a finger inside to tease her, Nick could feel her wetness coat his finger as he slid into her warmth. Angel gasped and threw back her head.

Nick quickly took advantage, pressing his hand deeper as he raised her up, her ass on his forearm. Angel squirmed, rubbing against him. Nick bent and sucked a nipple into his mouth, teasing it through the silk. He slid a finger in and out of her heat, lightly rubbing her clit with his thumb. Angel moaned and tightened around his finger. Pressing her close against him, Nick increased his thrusts.

He bit her nipple and was rewarded with a cry as Angel clamped down, drenching his hand as she came apart in his arms.

She placed her head against his shoulder, shivers running through her while her arms and legs tightened around him. Nick pulled his hand free from her warmth and licked his fingers clean, making smacking noises as he did.

"Pig."

It was so low Nick barely heard the comment. Nick chuckled as Angel giggled in his arms.

"Did you want another glass of champagne?"

Angel shook her head and squirmed against him.

Nick squeezed her to him, enjoying the feel of her, despite the tightness in his groin. "Are you ready for dinner? Or shall we just head straight to dessert?"

Angel raised her head to look at him, her eyes heavy lidded, a smirk teasing the corner of her lips.

Nick smiled in satisfaction. He may not have gotten his rocks off yet, but Angel was satisfied and that alone made his heart sing.

"I'm hungry. I hear the hotel restaurant has a Master Chef on staff."

Nick couldn't resist the look in her eyes, the glimmer of lust that he'd always wanted to see there. Nick leaned toward her, nibbling her neck, when her stomach growled.

"Hmm. I guess you are hungry." Nick carried her into his suite and straight through to the bathroom. "Let's get cleaned up a bit and head to dinner." He sat her on the counter and stepped back. Crossing his arms, Nick looked at her. "God, you look good enough to eat." At that, Angel's stomach growled again. Nick laughed while a blush worked its way up her neck to tint her cheeks an attractive pink.

Angel started to slide off of the counter, and Nick held her back. "Hold on, Angel." Nick grabbed a washcloth and got it warm and wet. Nick wagged his brows at her and gave her his best evil smile. "Spread 'em!"

"Hell, no!" Angel wiggled closer to the edge. "Help me down. I can do it." Nick grabbed her waist and settled her on her feet. Angel looked at him. "Aren't you leaving so I can get cleaned up a bit?"

"No." Nick snickered as she glared at him. When Nick didn't move Angel turned her back toward him, muttering under her breath. Nick laughed and washed his hands in the sink. He dried off and flipped a towel over her shoulder. "I'm more than willing to make sure you're nice and dry before we head down." Nick could see her neck getting red. He sure hoped it was embarrassment rather than anger. He'd better make sure. "I'm teasing, sweetheart."

Angel threw him an exasperated look over her shoulder. "Somehow I doubt that." She grabbed the towel and dried off. "Oh for Pete's sake, can you give me just a bit of privacy?" Angel turned and snapped the towel at him.

"Hey!" Nick laughed and grabbed it, tugging it out of her hands. "All right, you, knock it off. If you're hungry we better head out or we won't be leaving this room." Nick grabbed Angel and pulled her out of the bathroom.

"Slow down!" Angel was tugging her hand, trying to pull away.

Nick stopped. "Sorry. I'll make sure you don't have to say that again tonight." His grin was pure mischief. Angel rolled her eyes and laughed.

"Come on, let's go eat." Once again, the noise from her middle made itself known. "I was too nervous to eat earlier."

"After you." Nick held open the door to his room, escorting Angel out. "Wait. Do you need your crutches?"

"No. I just have to go slow." Nick grabbed her hand and they strolled to the elevator in a restful silence.

He nestled Angel in his arms as the elevator slowly descended. Nick took a deep breath and nuzzled her hair, gently kissing her neck as the doors opened.

"After you." Nick ushered Angel before him and then took her arm to escort her to the restaurant. The hostess led them to a secluded candle lit table, a perfect scene for seduction. Nick held out the chair, lending Angel a hand as she sat.

"Thank you." Angel gave him a smile, a little shy, but it warmed him all the way to his heart.

"You're welcome." Nick sat and they stared at each other before opening and perusing the menus the hostess had left with them. "Do you know what you would like?"

"Yes." Nick raised his hand to catch the waiter's attention.

They ordered and Nick sat back and couldn't keep it in anymore.

"How crazy is it that we ended up here together?"

Angel ducked her head. "It's unbelievable."

"It was meant to be."

Angel peeked up at him, her eyes glittering beneath her long lashes. "It just seems like such a huge coincidence."

Nick shook his head. "No. We are perfect for each other. Even the computer program agrees or we wouldn't be here."

Angel took a sip of her water. "How can you be sure?"

"We're combustible Angel. Didn't we just prove that?"

Nick enjoyed the flush that rose up her cheeks.

"There's more to a relationship than hot sex!"

"I know. Think of how well we got along at the hospital." Nick reached over and grasped her hands. "You can't say we don't know each other."

"Don't you think we're moving too fast?"

Nick released a hand and caressed the line of her jaw. "One thing I learned from Afghanistan is that you don't know how much time you have. Why waste it?"

Her mouth opened then closed. He chuckled, knowing Angel couldn't refute his logic.

She sniffed, tugged her hand from his and sat back in her chair.

Nick couldn't help but admire her creamy skin against the candy apple red of her dress. She looked good enough to eat.

"Stop staring at me like that."

"I can't help it. You're gorgeous. Everything I've ever dreamed of."

He heard her breath catch. Sitting back, happy and satisfied, Nick enjoyed the sight before him. Her porcelain skin flushed pinker and her nipples peaked beneath her dress. He was tempted to head back upstairs. Then Angel's stomach growled again.

"Damn. I guess I'll have to feed you instead of rushing you back upstairs."

Angel smirked, lifting her brow at him. "And who says I'd let you?"

Nick snorted and changed the subject. No need to wind himself up any more than he was. Just looking at her had him adjusting himself under the tablecloth.

"Tell me about the therapy you're here for."

Her snicker told him she wasn't fooled, but she let it go.

He and Angel talked throughout dinner, the sexual tension ratcheting higher as they learned more about each other. He didn't want to let Angel go. She fit him. She always had. Nick just hoped she felt the same way.

Their upbringings weren't that much different, both of them raised by their parents, who in this day and age were still married. They were both the eldest child and both had siblings. Nick's parents were both ex-military so they knew what Nick was getting into, even more than he had. Angel's, on the other hand, were not. Her father was a minister and her mom worked at a local big box store. When Angel had been wounded it had rocked their world, and not in a good way. Nick could understand. It had changed his life too.

Her parents didn't understand that Angel was still enlisted and that she still had orders to follow, albeit they were now from the military doctors. It was no wonder she had fled to the Chicago VA Hospital when there was an opening, even if it was at Christmas. The continuing pity and weeping would drive away a saint, let alone someone who was hurting and needed someone to lean on.

Nick knew he had to take her home with him. He wanted to take her home, needed to take her home with him. Nick would just have to persuade her.

The band began tuning up. The adjacent bar had a dance floor and Nick wanted to hold her. He turned to Angel. "Would you like to dance? Can you?"

"Yes, as long as we take it slow." Angel smiled at him. Nick signaled the waiter for the check and had it charged to his room. He stood and took her hand, helping her from the chair. Angel trailed behind him, fingers securely intertwined with his.

Leading her to the dance floor, the low level lighting gave it an intimate feel, Nick pulled Angel into his arms. Pulling her against him, swaying to the music, Nick kissed her. Her lips were soft and sweet, tasting of the coffee that had ended their meal. Nick nibbled at her mouth, sweeping his tongue inside to taste her. At her moan Nick pulled back and rested his head on top of hers and tightened his arms, sighing contentedly.

"I didn't expect you." Nick kissed the corner of her mouth, moving down her neck with a trail of kisses.

"Are you disappointed?" Nick raised his head and looked down into her eyes. What Nick saw there filled his heart.

"Never, Doc." Nick sighed, contented. "Did you know you were meeting me?"

"No." Angel hugged him closer. "I only knew that I was meeting someone named Nick."

Nick laughed. "I only knew I was meeting someone named Angelina." Nick kissed her. "I didn't know you would be my angel."

Angel laughed. "We both know that isn't true!"

Nick continued to sway with the music, Angel resting against him, her curves aligned perfectly with him, making him even harder. "You are to me. I didn't even think when that grenade flew over the sandbags. All that went through my mind was that you couldn't die. No matter what happened to me, you couldn't die. To be honest, I was at the point where it didn't matter to me if I lived or died."

Angel made a wounded sound and buried her head in his chest. "Don't ever say that." Nick hugged her tight. With her here, in his arms, Nick felt the peace he'd been searching for.

Nick licked Angel's ear. "You really are my angel. Would you like to take me on a tour of heaven?" He pulled her tighter against his groin, pressing his length against the softness of her body.

Angel pulled her shoulders back and shook her head. A crooked grin crossed her lips. "You are such a…" Angel laughed and laid her head on his chest.

"Hot, studly man? I'm so glad you think so." Nick squeezed her and Angel giggled. "Come on little girl." Nick waggled his brows at her. "I have some candy in my room. Come on up and pick out what you'd like." Nick started dancing them around the floor, heading toward the door way. Her laughter was encouraging and Nick danced them all the way to the elevator.

The short ride up was filled with sighs and murmurs, their bodies entwined. When the chime of the elevator announced their floor, they separated only to have Nick grab Angel for a long slow kiss. The doors started shutting and Nick cursed and pulled back, hitting the open button.

"Angel." His voice was hoarse, passion laden. "Come to my room with me?"

Angel looked at Nick. His face was taunt, eyes glittering darkly with passion. "Yes." Angel grinned, her eyes twinkling. "The dessert cart is there."

Nick gave a shout of laughter, the tension lightening. "Well, we can't skip dessert." Nick grabbed her hand and dragged her down the hall. He pulled out his key card and slid it in, pulling open the door. Nick ushered Angel in ahead of him and swung her up into his arms as the door clicked shut, her arms encircling his neck. Angel nuzzled him, the sensitive spot between his shoulder and neck, biting and laving the spot with her tongue. Nick shuddered, imagining that tongue on another part of his anatomy.

Nick carried her further into his suite, past the Christmas tree and into the bedroom. Laying her across the bed, her golden hair spread on the amber bedspread, Angel looked like a disheveled angel. Nick stripped off his shirt, toed off his shoes and dropped his pants. Her eyes widened as his erection sprang toward his belly. She grinned naughtily.

"Commando?" Angel asked playfully.

Nick smiled and without saying a word, stripped her dress from her, exposing her body to his view. Angel made to cover herself, but Nick stopped her, leaning forward to grab her hands with his.

"I'm not the only one who went commando." Nick's eyes ran across her body, a smirk on his lips. He crawled on the bed, laying on top of her and breathed in her scent, running his tongue over her throat. Whispering softly as he did. "Angel, you being here, being the one to meet me is like a gift I had only dreamed of having."

Nick burrowed into her neck, sucking at the spot where her neck and shoulder met and licked his way to her clavicle. Angel gasped. Nick continued lower. His tongue outlining her areola and flicking her hardened nipple. His hand grasped her breast, plumping it up to his mouth. Nick continued teasing her until she squirmed. Then he pinched her nipple between his thumb and forefinger as his mouth whispered over to its twin.

Angel moaned as he suckled her nipple, arching toward him. The sounds his angel made drove him wild. She managed to maneuver her hands so that she could reach him. Nick moaned releasing her breast.

"Ah, Angel." Nick kissed his way back to her neck to nibble on her ear. "Sweetheart." Her hands were busy, caressing him. Nick pulled back and looked at her, notching his cock into her softness. Not penetrating, Nick would never do anything to cause her harm, but settling her warmth and wetness against him. Nick rubbed his chest against her breasts, her nipples hardening even more.

"Why are you stopping?" Angel looked at him, a hint of uncertainty in her eyes.

"Because the condoms are on the nightstand and if I move…"

Angel laughed and wiggled away from him, sucking in a breath and shivering as his cock slid over her clit when she moved up. Nick moaned and rested his head against her belly as she wiggled her way up even more.

Nick looked up. Angel's face glowed as she stretched further and grasped the box by the edge. Angel crowed in triumph. "Got 'em!" She pulled them toward her and gasped as Nick buried his head between her legs. Angel's shimmying and wiggling had moved her up, so that it wasn't her belly, but her pussy he was facing. He slid his hands down her legs. His hand touched the top of her prosthetic. Angel jerked away and froze. Nick glanced up and shifted his hands back, spreading her legs wider, exposing her glistening folds. Nick knew that would have to be addressed another time. But not now. Now it was time to take what he thought he'd never have.

He licked her, delving inside to lap up the cream flowing from her. Her squeak had him burying his face against her and his tongue licking deep inside. Her swollen clit was begging for attention and the tips of her breasts were diamond hard.

Nick filled his hands with her breasts, his fingers playing with her nipples. Pulling back and gently blowing across her pussy, the warm air caused her to moan and undulate toward his face. Nick delicately licked her, avoiding the nub she was serving up to him. Angel moaned and arched toward his mouth. Chuckling and pressing the flat of his tongue against her lower lips elicited another whimper from Angel.

He sat up on his knees and yanked her down toward him, fastening his mouth on her breast and sucking it in in a rhythmic pull that had her wailing and arching toward him. Nick lay down against her, his hard abdomen against her hot and slippery pussy, to keep her hands from touching herself. The pressure of his body just enough to keep her from rubbing against him. Her breath hitched, and her arms wrapped around him, fingers tunneling in his hair as she offered herself up to him.

With one hand Nick grabbed a condom. He grinned. They were now strewn all over the bed. He released her breast and kissed his way down her body. His tongue circled her belly button, fondling the gem dangling there. Sexy, Nick thought, and gave it a little tug.

Nick moved lower, over her pussy again. He exhaled and watched Angel shiver as his warm breath moved across her. Opening the condom, he slid it on while slowly licking her, tickling her opening with the tip of his tongue. He separated her lips with his fingers, giving him a luscious view of her begging, glistening snatch.

Nick slid a finger, and then two inside her. She was so fucking tight. Angel arched, hands grabbing his hair painfully. Sliding them in and out, he watched her body grasping them. Moving faster, Nick leaned over and sucked her clit into his mouth. She arched then wailed, her body clamping down on his fingers. God, she was hotter than the recoil blast from a rocket launcher!

Nick withdrew his hand and slid up her body. He centered his shaft over her creamy cunt and slid balls deep inside of her. He stilled. It felt like the final piece of a puzzle settling into place. Tears stung his eyes. He moved, slowly, in and out, enjoying the feel of her tight flesh surrounding him. She cried out, spasms shaking her body. He pumped faster and faster, her cries increasing until her body bowed as a sharp scream left her lips. Nick kissed her then, long and deep as his body released into her warmth, his shaft pulsing, filling the condom as he shook from the strength of his reaction.

He collapsed above her, his weight holding her boneless body to the mattress. A groan escaped him as he began to slide out of her body. Her arms tightened around him, holding him to her, in her.

"I don't want to crush you, Angel."

"You're not."

"I'm so glad it was you on the balcony, Doc." Nick kissed her, slow and deep. Her moan made his chest tighten. "I realized how much you meant to me when I thought I had lost you without ever having you."

Angel smiled at him, contentment in her features. "I didn't want to be your rebound, Saint," she said softly. "I knew what happened. Everyone knew your girl had broken up with you."

"Never that, Angel, the grenade opened my eyes real fast. Facing death has a way of doing that." Nick slowly kissed her neck, running his tongue along the crease, the slight tang of her perspiration sweeter than honey.

She shivered. "MADWebs was my shot at trying to forget you." She sounded breathless.

Nick laughed. "Mine too." He laid his head against hers. "It's been rough. The nightmares were driving me out of my mind." Nick sighed, "I realized I wasn't going to be able to do it all on my own. I've been getting help, talking to a fucking shrink." Nick laughed. "He's the one who recommended that I sign up for this."

Angel groaned as he rubbed his chest against her nipples. The tightening buds had him salivating to taste her.

"You think that's bad? I swear to God my physical therapist is a Drill Instructor! I'd rather go through all that touchy, feely crap than be worn to a nub every day."

"Touchy, feely crap? I'll give you touchy, feely crap!" Nick pulled back, out of her warmth and started tickling her. "Touchy feely crap my ass!"

Angel's giggles filled the room, the joy in them making him smile.

"Stop! Fine. Uncle!" Nick laughed and gave her a hug, his weight pressing her into the bed.

"Here, let's clean up." Nick stood to remove the condom. "How about a snack? There's a whole dessert cart going to waste out there." Nick gestured toward the balcony.

"Mmm, I hope they have chocolate mousse." Angel grasped his hand to pull up, swinging her legs over the side of the bed. "I could use another shower."

"I'm willing to share." Nick leaned over and gave her a kiss.

Angel pushed him toward the bathroom. "Go. I'm a little slower."

Nick kissed the top of her head. "Don't be too long." He headed to the bathroom.

Angel could hear the toilet flush and the water run in the shower.

Nick stuck his head out. "Hey, are you coming?"

"No. I'll take a shower when you're done."

Nick stared at her.

Angel stared back, lifting a brow. "Go. I'll sit right here until you're done."

Nick looked at her and shook his head. "Why?"

"Because." Angel shooed him with a wave of her hands. "Go."

Nick sighed and ducked back in the bathroom. He had been looking forward to soaping her up. He wondered why Angel didn't want to take a shower with him, and then grinned. Maybe she knew that it wasn't only showering on his mind. Nick quickly cleaned up and turned off the water, grabbing a towel and drying off as he headed back to the bedroom and Angel.

Angel stretched and tried to stand. Nick tossed the towel on the bed and headed toward her. "Hey, need any help?"

"No, I can do it alone. I need to use the head too." She raised a brow at him. "Got a problem with that?"

"Nope. Need your crutches?"

"No. I'm supposed to be getting used to my new leg." Angel pushed up and sat back down with at groan. Grimacing, she put her hands out to him. "I think was on my feet too long. Help me stand?"

Nick grabbed her hands and pulled her up and into him. Her soft silky warmth had him at attention again.

Angel snickered. "Got a problem, Corporal?"

"Hey, I'm just showing respect to a superior!" Nick laughed. "My own private salute." She rolled her eyes at him.

"Fine. Now let me try this on my own." Angel pushed him away, her hand accidentally sliding across his 'flagpole'. Nick saw her smirk, maybe not so accidentally! He started to follow her. "Don't hover. I get enough of that from my family."

Nick stood back, ready to jump to her aid if necessary. He watched her slowly make her way to the bathroom, limping only slightly. She grasped the door frame and smiled back at him. The joy in her face, at her accomplishment, filled him with pride.

"You made it, Angel." Nick knew his pride in her showed in his face. "There is a bathrobe on the back of the door, unless you want to eat naked on the balcony."

"No, I don't think that's a good idea, no matter how many heaters they have out there!" Angel went all the way in and shut the door.

Nick laughed knowing Angel was probably rolling her eyes at him. Pulling a pair of sweat pants from his suitcase, he put them on. The shower started and Nick prowled the room, wanting to join her, but knowing it probably wasn't time, yet.

The sliding door leading to the balcony afforded a spectacular view. The city glowed with multi colored lights and Christmas Carols could be heard faintly on the breeze. Nick loved this season. It was one of the reasons the guys called him Saint Nick. Chuckling, Nick thought of the arrangements he had made for all the guys that didn't head home for the holidays. His surprise should be jumping out of the cake in the lounge about this time tomorrow night, jingle bells and all. The shower turned off and Nick turned toward the bathroom door.

* * * *

Angel smirked at the look of eagerness in Saint's eyes as she ran her fingers across his hardness. She laughed, closing the bathroom door in his face. Her abdomen clenched in desire. Angel tingled, wanting to once again feel Saint's hardness filling her. If she let him in she wouldn't get clean. The ache in her leg was another reason all together.

Angel needed a shower. Regardless of how tempting it was to have Saint come in and wash her back, Angel needed to do this by herself. She needed the heat of the shower on her leg, and she didn't want to take her prosthetic off in front of him.

Angel flipped down the toilet seat and sat. She unbuckled the leg, grabbing it with both hands and setting it on the sink vanity. Next she rolled down the protective liner. Shuddering she gazed at what was left. Her leg was healing, though red scars crisscrossed her skin. Shiny in places and, Angel's lips tightened, ugly, just ugly to look at. Bruises from her prosthetic marred her skin, the obvious grafts from multiple surgeries were plain to see.

Taking a deep breath, determined to keep her tears from falling from her stinging eyes, Angel tossed her liner on the vanity. Her stump tingled as her circulation once again flowed easier with the liner off. She didn't want it wet. The others she had were in her suitcase, in her room. She wouldn't, couldn't let Saint see her without her leg. It would be obvious that she wasn't a whole woman anymore.

Logically she knew that Saint knew that, but the tightness in her chest whenever she thought of him seeing her without her peg leg convinced her that she was right. The last thing she wanted was for him to see how much of a mess she really was. This night, this blind date had been all about building her confidence back up, not giving away her heart.

Standing up, Angel shook her head. Like her room, this bathroom was handicapped accessible. She grabbed the vanity and hopped closer to the shower. Reaching out with one hand she grabbed one of the bars in the shower. Shifting her weight, she hopped in the shower area, grabbing another bar when she was close enough, balancing on her one leg. Leaning over to turn the shower on was trickier.

Her nostrils flared and Angel took a steadying breath, her knuckles white as she squeezed the safety bars. She ignored that fact that her leg just hung there, useless. She refused to dwell on it. Angel loosened her hands, keeping them tight enough to hold her weight, but loose enough that she was no longer losing circulation in her fingers. She drew another deep breath and slowly let it out.

The warmth of the water beating down on her loosened the tightness in her muscles. Angel sighed. Relaxing her shoulders, it brought other aches alive. Her nipples tingled and her groin was tender. A smile slipped across her face, thinking of why.

Her leg started to shake and Angel turned, sitting down on the bench provided. Her eyes widened at the chill of the tile beneath her cheeks. Releasing the bars, she grabbed the washcloth and shower gel that were in easy reach.

Angel flushed, her eyes sparkling as she realized that Saint must have left them there for her. The shower also was adjusted so that it easily reached where she was sitting. Happiness flooded her soul, her heart captivated by the unspoken care. Angel gulped a breath and the tears that edged her eyes fell.

Wiping her face with the cloth, Angel wiped away her tears. She'd done enough crying. Regardless of the fact that they were tears of happiness, they brought too many memories of her despair. Angel was determined to laugh, to let out the burst of happiness in her soul. Her heart raced just thinking of Saint.

Soaping up, the cloth was rough on her tender bits. Thinking of Saint's mouth, her nipples peaked. Her groin clenched, moisture gathering just thinking about his talented mouth, fingers and other bits. Angel relaxed, a smile on her face and let the warm water rinse away the soap and let all her negative thoughts drain away. Tonight, away from the family that, though they loved her, drove her nuts, she could live again.

Taking a deep breath and letting it out, Angel smiled and stretched. The water streamed down on her and Angel groaned, leaning forward. Her muscles had been sore from her PT. They were really sore from her workout with Saint. A sigh escaped her. She hadn't felt so deliciously tired in a long time.

Stretching her arms, Angel took a deep breath. It was time to get out. Leaning forward, holding on to one of the bars, she turned off the shower. She swore she could hear Saint breathing through the door.

Angel turned and pulled down a towel from the rack next to the shower. Everything was in easy reach. She was glad that both her room and Saint's had handicapped bathrooms. It made it so much easier to be independent when she could reach everything without help. The shower stall could easily accommodate a wheel chair also. Not many hotels had that. Most had the bare minimum space required by law if they even had handicapped accommodations.

Wrapping one towel around her head, Angel grabbed another for her body. She dried off as much as she could from the bench. Standing up, she maneuvered back to the toilet, grabbing her liner for her prosthetic along the way.

Sitting down, she pulled it on. Angel cursed and took it off again. Any dampness made it hell to get on. The humidity in the air despite the fan left a thin residue of water over everything, including her. She redried her leg. Pulling the liner back on, it slid into place. Angel smoothed it over her stump, having learned from experience that it couldn't have any lumps or twists and turns. If it did, it wouldn't let the prosthesis seat properly and would cause sores if left.

"Did you want any clothes from your room?" Angel ignored Saint. His well-meaning question was just pushing to get her back out there. Angel needed to center herself. Saint kept her emotions roiling. Angel didn't know if that was a good thing or not. For now, she would ignore him. She'd get her clothes when she was done.

Angel reached over and grabbed for her leg; it slipped out of her grasp. Letting fall another curse, Angel stood and grabbed the leg, sitting back down as she brought it over. Seating it and hearing it click in place, she winced. Her leg began throbbing. She knew she'd done too much.

She stood, seating it firmly. Ignoring the pain, Angel limped to the door.

Her eyes widened at the size of the bathrobe on the hook. She'd have to be a giant to wear it properly. Shrugging, Angel pulled it on. She laughed and wrapped it around herself. It practically went around her twice. Angel tied the sash around her waist. She had no clue how she would even walk in it. Hell, she could hardly walk anyway.

"This ought to be fun."

Angel opened the door and rolled her eyes at the laughter on Saint's face when he looked her over from head to toe.

Chapter Six

"Did you want any clothes from your room?" Nick hollered through the closed door. Nick could hear Angel moving around, but no answer. A bit of cussing came from the other room and he grinned.

The door slowly opened and his grin widened. Angel was buried in the large robe. She looked like a little girl playing dress up.

"Could you get me some sweats? I don't think I'll be able to safely walk with this on." Angel stepped out, the robe dragging on the floor, impeding her steps. Nick picked her up and sat her on the bed. Her squeak of surprise had him grinning.

"No problem." Nick kissed her on the nose and headed to the connecting door. It was unlocked. "You mean I could have gone in and had my way with you earlier?" Nick had a wicked grin on his face.

"No. It was locked on my side until I was ready to come over."

"Party pooper."

Angel giggled, a sound Nick wanted to hear more of.

"Go get me some clothes, Corporal."

Nick laughed, happy with his world and did as his angel requested.

Grabbing her clothes from the suitcase, Nick looked around. Angel's crutches were the only thing out of place. They were tossed in the corner onto the floor. Nick went over and moved them next to the connecting door. That way if she needed them, they were handy. He headed back to his room.

Nick tried to help Angel dress, but she shoved him away. He might have really done more to impede her than help, but how was he supposed to ignore all that silky skin? When he'd knelt to help put her sweats on, her pussy lips were there, lips pouting, just begging for his kiss. Was it his fault he liked to French? Seeing the glistening flesh, Nick dove back in, ignoring Angel's halfhearted attempts to stop him.

At her broken cry, his tongue was rewarded with her sweet juices. *God, he was ready to explode!*

"Jeez, Saint, enough!" Angel's voice was breathless, words contradicting the shaking of her body.

Nick ignored her words, his tongue still licking her clean. Nick stopped when her shudders ended, scraping his teeth over her pussy as he pulled away. "Okay." Nick gave a big theatrical sigh. "I know when to surrender." He snickered. She still didn't have any clothes on.

Angel pushed him away, looking flustered.

Nick ran his hands over her legs, stopping at her prosthetic. Nick looked up at her. "How is it healing?"

"Fine." Angel glanced at him and looked away.

"Angel."

"It hurts, okay. I hate it." Angel had tears in her eyes. "I don't want to talk about it."

"Why haven't you taken it off?" Nick cocked his head at her. "Is that why you didn't want me to shower with you?"

"I don't want you to see it."

"Why not? I was the one that put the tourniquet on your leg. I was there, Angel. I saw it in the worst shape it's ever going to be."

"It's ugly. I don't want you to see how horrible it is."

Nick's heart ached. The strongest, most beautiful woman Nick knew was crying. Why? Because he was an insensitive pig. But, he knew it was critical to address this issue.

"Angel, everything about you is beautiful." Nick guided her face to look at him. "Everything, Angel." He lifted Angel up and sat on the bed, cuddling her in his lap. He ran his hands up and down her back. "There is nothing about it that is ugly. Your scars are a badge of courage. Your bravery is amazing."

"It's still ugly. How can you even want me?"

Nick wiggled his hips under her. "Uh, Angel? Does this feel like I don't want you?"

Angel laughed, a little watery, but better. "Hmm?"

"No." Angel sat up and straddled him, "But you haven't seen it."

Nick sighed and closed his eyes, his hands holding her to him. He knew he'd be in trouble for what he said next. "Angel, this may sound crude, but I wouldn't give a shit if you had no legs, as long as I could fuck you." Nick braced himself at her gasp. The smack across his head was harder than expected. Tightening his arms so Angel couldn't get loose, he opened his eyes.

Yup, Angel was glaring at him and still wriggling to get away. Nick grinned at her and laughed. "Gotcha."

"You are a pig." Angel was still glaring, but had stopped trying to get away. Then Angel laughed. "You really are a pig." Angel leaned against him, arms around his neck. "How the hell did you get the nickname Saint?"

Nick lay back on the bed pulling her on top of him. He ran his hands along her back and buttocks, enjoying her silky smoothness, pulling his angel back down to his chest as she struggled to sit up. "Stay here and I'll tell you." Angel settled on top of him. "Well, it's not any secret. For one thing, my name is Santiago, as you well know."

Angel snorted. "Duh."

"Hush you. You wanted to know. So the guys shortened it to Saint in boot camp." Nick laughed, running his hands down her legs, playing with the top of the sleeve that covered her prosthetic. "After we were out in the field, they swore I was the opposite of a saint with my behavior so it stuck. Saint's the biggest sinner." Nick smiled. "Plus, every Christmas I'd hang those cheap, little stockings up in our barracks with gag gifts in them for all the guys in my unit. Since my first name is Nicholas, they'd tease me and call me Saint Nicholas. I guess it was a combination that stuck."

"I guess you didn't do anything this year, huh?" Angel asked. "Since you're here."

Nick snickered. "You're wrong there. I managed to make arrangements for a special cake to be delivered on Christmas Eve. One of the strippers from Anchor's Away is going to jump out of it."

"They'll get in so much trouble if anyone reports it!" Angel's eyes were wide as she shook her head.

Nick laughed.

"Yeah, but who'd be stupid enough to report it?" Nick rolled over, putting Angel beneath him. "I'm tired of talking." He leaned down and kissed her.

Her arms came around his neck.

He savored the softness of her lips before tasting the sweetness of her mouth.

Angel's hands ran across his chest and around to his back, and then down, inside the band of his sweatpants, pushing them down.

Nick helped, shoving and then kicking them off. His breath caught at the feel of her in his arms, the silkiness of her skin against him everywhere.

"Angel." It's all Nick said. All he could say. He reached for another condom and ripped it open, sliding out of her arms to put it on.

Angel grabbed it from his hand and slowly rolled it on his length.

He moaned and watched a smile flit across her face.

Moving back onto his knees on the bed, he looked down at her legs. Angel's smile faltered.

"Don't."

"Angel, you need to know it doesn't matter." Nick leaned down, kissed her neck and continued nibbling his way down her body. He laid his head on her abdomen, kissing it before his hands slowly rolled down the sleeve on her leg. He looked up at Angel. "Is there a trick to this?"

"No." Angel sighed and sniffled. "Kinda." Nick rolled his eyes.

"That was clear."

"Stop." Angel tugged at him.

"Nope. I'm gonna show you it doesn't matter." Nick kissed her leg above the liner. "How does it come off?"

"You're not going to stop are you?"

Nick shook his head.

"Fine." Angel pushed him away until he was standing in front of her. "Let me show you." Angel sat up and glanced at him. Nick watched as she reached down. She clicked a pin near the ankle and pulled down, removing her plastic leg.

Nick looked at her leg and pointed. "What's this?"

"It's the pin that holds the leg on. See?" Angel showed him the inside of the prosthetic. "It locks into this socket. So the leg won't come off."

Nick reached for the liner with the pin still on her leg.

Angel scowled and slapped his hands away. "Let me." Angel slowly rolled down the liner on her leg, looking at him before she had it completely off. "Are you sure?"

Nick leaned over and kissed her. "Yes, now hurry up."

Angel sighed heavily and rolled the liner all the way off. She kept her head down as she tossed it on the nightstand.

"Hmm." Nick said nothing more until Angel looked up, uncertainty in her eyes before she once again dropped her gaze. "Well, it looks a lot better than the last time I saw it. It's not mangled and spraying blood." Nick heard a watery giggle. "It *is* naked. I like naked."

Angel lifted her head and smiled at him.

Nick grabbed Angel and pushed her to her back, crawling over her, shuffling around until they both lay in center of the big bed, his knees between her spread thighs.

"I really like naked." Nick leaned down and kissed her. "I really, really like naked." His voice was hoarse.

Nick kissed his way down her body, stopping to tease her nipples until Angel cried out, her hands grasping the comforter as she squirmed beneath him. He continued down, circling her belly button with kisses and slow licks. He kissed and caressed his way lower, teasing the sensitive creases of her legs with his breathe, and turned to dip his tongue in her slit, tasting her cream as Angel squirmed. Nick licked deeper, enjoying the feel of the fluttering walls of her cunt on his tongue as he teased her. His thumb lightly stroked her clit, causing her breath to catch her and her hands to press his head harder against her. Nick chuckled, knowing the vibrations would add to the sensations Angel was feeling.

She moaned and spread her legs wider, inviting him to delve deeper. His tongue swiped along her slit, his hands moving to her buttocks, tilting her toward his mouth. Nick licked her, a long slow stroke of his tongue, ending at her clit where he delicately nibbled, watching it swell. Giving her clit a light kiss, he pulled away, sliding out from beneath her hands and continued to lick his way down her thigh, kissing the slight impression left by the sleeve on her delicate skin.

Nick's hands slowly stroked her leg. Kneeling above her, Nick could see the scarring was minimal, the skin smooth and shiny where the stitches had been made. She had lost her foot and most of her leg below her knee. Nick kissed her stump and bowed his head. He swallowed and looked up at Angel, a suspicious shimmer in his eyes.

"I'm sorry I didn't protect you enough."

Angel reached out to him, grasping his arms. "No. If it wasn't for you I would be dead." They met together in a desperate kiss, Angel's arms went around his neck and she leaned back pulling him over her as she lay down on the bed. Nick resisted, leaning on his arms, looking down at her. "Please, Saint. I need you."

"Angel." Nick nibbled on the soft flesh of her neck, flexed and slid home giving in to the desire and desperation he felt. They both moaned. Angel shivered and he dropped his forehead against hers. She wrapped her arms around him, sliding her hands to the small of his back, nails scoring lightly against him. Nick pumped into her, hard and fast.

Nick leaned back, grabbed and spread Angel's thighs hooking her good leg over his broad shoulders and holding the thigh of her injured leg against him. The move let him sink deeper into her, her passage hot and tight around him. She moaned as Nick sank deeper. Looking into her eyes, he turned his head and kissed her thigh, watching her eyes darken.

Angel arched, hands grasping at his ass and pulling him into her. "Move, dammit."

Nick watched her shiver.

"Saint, move!"

Nick laughed. "Aye aye, Doc." He leaned forward and quickened his pace, slamming home again and again. He could feel her tighten around him. Running his hands under her, he could feel the tremble of her legs, the grasping of her pussy on his cock as he caressed her. He kissed her thigh and sliding one hand to her pussy pressed against her clit with his thumb.

Angel screamed and clamped down on his dick. He threw back his head and moaned, shooting into her as she pulsed around him. A shiver ran through her body as the last of his load filled the condom, her pussy clinging to his cock.

"Oh," Angel panted. "My. God." Angel's voice was breathless. "I think I've died of pleasure." Before Nick could speak, a growl came from her belly. Nick laughed.

"Nope." Nick kissed Angel, letting her legs down. "But I think I might be starving you to death. I didn't think you ate enough at dinner." Nick rolled over and sat up. "Come on, dessert's on the balcony." He disposed of the condom in the waste basket and turned around.

Angel was sprawled against the bed. Her silky soft skin glistening as she lay there.

Nick smiled and walked toward her leaning over to kiss her where she lay.

"Come on lazy, up and at 'em." Nick grabbed her hands and pulled her until she sat up. "How about a quick shower, Angel?"

Angel groaned and flopped back on the bed pulling a pillow over her head.

Nick laughed. "Fine." He went into the bathroom and turned on the faucet. Nick grabbed a washcloth and put it under the warm water. Twisting the excess water from it and grabbing a dry towel Nick headed back into the bedroom.

Angel squeaked when the warmth of the washcloth touched her. "What do you think you're doing?"

"Just lay there, Angel." Nick washed the evidence of their passion from between her thighs. "God, you're beautiful, Angel."

When he had her washed, Nick swiped the cloth around his cock quickly before tossing it toward the bathroom. Taking the towel Nick patted her dry. His angel must be tired. She didn't even fight him over cleaning her up. Nick pulled her pants from the floor and pulled them over her foot. "Lift up."

Angel groaned and lifted her hips.

Nick leaned over and gave her silky tummy a quick raspberry. Her breathless laugh had him smiling as he finished sliding her pants up. Nick leaned over and grabbed her sweatshirt next. "Come on, raise those arms."

"I can put my sweatshirt on." Angel tried battling his hands as Nick pulled it over her head. "Where is my bra by the way?"

Nick dressed her quickly, despite her halfhearted struggles. "You didn't ask for one."

Angel glared at him, his smirk telling her all she needed to know. Nick grabbed his sweats from the corner of the bed where they had landed.

"So, you have two choices. I carry you to the table or I can get your crutches."

"Get my crutches." Angel looked at him. "Or I could put my leg back on." Nick shook his head.

"I know darn well that's a new leg. You're only supposed to have it on for a short time to get used to it."

"So get my crutches already, Mr. Expert. I'm still hungry. I was so nervous, dinner is the only meal I ate today." The rumble from her middle bore out her statement, making them both smile.

"Your wish is my command, Angel." Nick entered the adjoining room and came back out with her gear. "Here you go." Nick helped her up, holding the crutches until Angel was steady.

"Thanks."

He placed his hand at the small of her back to guide her over the frame of the sliding door. At the table Nick pulled back her chair to seat her, kissing her neck and placing her crutches against the rail before heading to the dessert cart. Lifting up the lid Nick looked over the selections.

"So, Angel, what'll it be? Looks like we have cheesecake with chocolate sauce and raspberries, chocolate mousse, makings for sundaes, mmm. Pumpkin pie, banana cream pie, French silk, Tiramisu. I think I've died and gone to heaven."

"I'll take the chocolate mousse."

Nick grabbed the dish and, bowing to Angel, placed it on the plate in front of her.

"Mad'mozelle ees zerved."

Angel laughed at his phony French accent.

"A cup of coffee will be just ze ting to go with our desserts." Nick smiled at Angel. "Would Mad'mozelle like a cup?"

"Yes, please." Angel smiled at Nick. She looked content. It was a good look for her. One he intended to keep on her face.

Nick kissed her softly, and then poured a cup of coffee for both of them before sitting down.

The desserts were delicious, the cart keeping them chilled, but not frozen despite the temperature outside. The twinkling lights and the Christmas Carols made the evening magical. Nick finished and sat back with a well satisfied sigh.

"How come you flew to the VA over Christmas? What about your family?"

Angel sighed. "My parents were driving me crazy. I couldn't even breathe by myself. My mom looks at me and cries. My dad tries to make everything easier. They're fighting, and it's over me. Why? I don't know." Angel took a sip of coffee. "They both want me to get out of the

Navy, but I still have a year left on my enlistment. I'm not sure what I'll do then."

"That sucks." Nick looked into his coffee cup. "My parents don't even know I was wounded. I wouldn't let the hospital call them." Nick heard the click of her cup as it hit the saucer and winced.

"What? Why? How come you never told them?" Angel watched as Nick carefully set down his cup. "I thought you were close to your parents."

"Yes. I am." Nick ran his hands through his hair. "If I had told them, my mom would have been on the first plane out. They worry enough. I know my mom does." He laughed. "She claims her gray hair is all because of me. My dad's a little mellower, but he'd have been with her."

"They wouldn't have let them on base."

"Uh, my mom probably wouldn't have let that stop her. They'd have found a way. They're both veterans and would have used that to get on."

"Would that have been so bad?"

"They couldn't really afford it, and I knew I was going to be okay. I knew I needed to spend some time at home when this tour ended, but I needed to be alone then." Nick looked at her, the twinkling Christmas bulbs highlighting her delicate features. Nick knew his parents would be okay when they found out. Mom would be mad at first, but she wouldn't worry as he'd be right in front of her, healthy and whole. Nick decided a change of subject was in order. "Why didn't you answer my letters?"

Her eyes widened and then dropped. "I didn't want pity letters or a relationship based on pity. I know you were just trying to keep my spirits up."

"Yeah, because I get a fucking hard on when I pity someone." Nick rolled his eyes. "Do you still think I pity you? Look at you. You have one hell of a weapon. Snap the foot off and whack someone with it and step on them with the spike at the bottom. You'd have them down in a matter of seconds."

"Oh my God! You are such a...such a Marine! Everything is a weapon." Angel was laughing. "You are such an idiot!"

Nick grinned at her. "Love me anyway?"

Angel looked at him, a smile still curving her lips and a sparkle in her eye. "Yes. Love you anyway."

"So, Angel, what are your plans for Christmas?" Nick was watching her.

Her eyes widened at his question.

"You did say you loved me. So, come home with me. I'm done playing games. I want you. I want you to meet my family." Nick heard the bells of a clock tolling midnight, its sound competing with the carols and the never ending traffic noise of Chicago.

He could see the uncertainty filling her. The look in her eyes and in the way she started fidgeting at the table made her trepidation clear.

Nick flashed a grin at her. "It's Christmas Eve. I did unwrap you and I don't give up my presents. If you don't believe me, you'll just have to ask my parents, which means you have to meet them."

Angel snorted, mirth edging out the uncertainty in her eyes. "Good one. I don't have to do anything I don't want to do."

"But you do want to, don't you?" Nick's voice was serious.

Angel looked at him.

Nick gazed earnestly into her eyes. His heart shown in his, Nick knew it did. He watched Angel and finally saw the uncertainty die, and happiness blossom her eyes.

"Yes," Angel whispered, "I want to."

He stood and pulled Angel into his embrace. "I love you Angel."

She looked into his eyes, hers sparkling back at him. A smile graced her face. "I love you, Saint."

"Does that mean you'll come with me to meet my parents?"

"Are you sure?" Angel glanced down at her leg. "What will they think?"

Nick nuzzled the top of her head. "That I picked the perfect woman for me. So, will you go with me? Meet my parents? Share my life?"

Her arms tightened around him. "Yes."

Nick pulled her up, bringing Angel's lips to his. The sound of traffic died away, everything but the angel in his arms falling away from his consciousness.

"But I have to be back on the twenty sixth." Angel whispered against his lips.

Nick pulled back. "That isn't much of a life."

She smiled. "But it's my life. I have to meet with the doctor." Her smile dropped. "That's probably going to be my life for a while."

"No problem. We'll spend Christmas with my family and drive back down here that morning. Go back up when we can." Nick stroked the nape of her neck. He couldn't stop touching her.

"I've probably got therapy and evaluations."

Nick backed up, holding Angel at arm's length. "Angel, are you trying to talk me or you out of this?"

"No." Angel shook her head. "I just want you to know what you're getting into."

Nick growled. "I know what I'm getting. The perfect woman for me." He pulled her back against him. "No matter what, we'll face the future together."

"I love you."

Nick pulled her tight against him. Her every curve fitted perfectly against him.

Angel wrapped her arms around his neck, pulling his lips to hers.

He could feel the last of the darkness leave, the hole inside him filled with joy and hope for the future. Their future, together.

THE END

About the Author

Beverly Ovalle dabbled with writing on and off for years when her best friend finally dared her to submit a story to a writing contest. Beverly decided she had nothing to lose and since she'd always wanted to be an author sent it in and agonized for months waiting to hear back. Contract in hand she has never looked back.

Beverly has been obsessed with dragons and romance since she was a young girl, collecting dragon books and reading everything she could find on them even down to the care of real life dragons. She's always been slightly panicked that the world as we know it will end, so has prepped for it, haunting survivalist pages and prepper projects she felt she needed in the event SHTF.

An avid fan of all romance, Beverly's goal is to share her love of the written word and write the hot and erotic romances that she enjoys. She writes what she loves to read and it was only a matter of time before her obsessions crept into her writing for her to share. She hopes you enjoy her tales as much as she loves writing them.

A Navy Veteran, Beverly has traveled around the world and the United States enabling her to bring her settings to life, meeting and marrying her husband of twenty-five years along the way for her own romance. Reading romances since the fourth grade she's followed as the genre changed and spread into the vast cornucopia of romance offered today.

Other books by Beverly Ovalle:

Stealing Hope

Amazon Bestseller in Erotica Paranormal AND Erotica Science Fiction

The apocalypse has come and gone.
Those who survived learned to adapt.
Dragons awaken to once again reign over the skies.

Upon eruption of a volcano, Ari awakens to a changed world, and a knowing that his dragon's mate is near. He saves her twice—once as a dragon, and again as a man—and wins her confidence.

Hope cried out, moaning, "just change me with pleasure?"

Hope is restless and unfulfilled until she meets Ari, the man of her fantasies. The sensual tension between them heightens with every touch. When their passion explodes, Hope gets pulled into the dragon's mating ritual...and into a world of erotic sensation she never dreamed existed but now cannot live without. The dragon binds his mate to him with a ritual that shows Hope her true nature in this humorous erotic romance.

Love Me Forever

Staff Sergeant Liam McGregor doesn't know what hit him. Sent home to recuperate from an IED blast, Liam is stuck in a wheelchair and is sentenced to surgery and physical therapy before he can walk again.

A physical therapist, Abby Worth has loved Liam McGregor since she first noticed boys. It's too bad he's her brother's best friend. She has always been firmly put in the baby sister zone no matter how hard she tried to catch his eye.

Liam sees Abby and when she goes home with him doesn't know how he can keep his hands off of her. She's now old enough to touch and the fire in his blood and the combination of pain killers make him lose control. Abby can't help but take what she's always wanted.

Together they have to overcome their fear of being left behind to grab what they have always wanted-each other.

Triple D Dude Ranch

Blaire is a freelance photographer on assignment. She is heading home to Texas, armed with her camera to do a photo feature for the Tribune. Taking photos of the dude ranch, she gets an eyeful of an uninhibited cowboy through her lens. The summer heat of Texas has nothing on the heat he generates in her.

Dan was expecting a photographer but not the sexy urban cowgirl that arrived. He knew it was hot out, he just hadn't expected the hot and sexy woman to make him burn the minute he caught sight of her. One look and he had to quench this fire inside.

One touch between Dan and Blaire sparks a wildfire that burns hotter than the Texas summer and is just as hard to put out.

Lightning Strike

For generations Levi's family had guarded a sacred glen in the mountains. Still far from man this isolated area was a favorite spot of his grandfather. Levi grew up listening to his tales and fell in love without ever having stepped foot there.

Now Levi's family, led by his grandmother, wanted to sell the land. With only his grandfather and Levi against it, Levi has to prove to the rest of the family why they needed to continue their guardianship. Believing in his grandfather's tales despite himself, Levi went armed with his camera and his well-known expertise behind the lens and headed out for proof.

Providing that proof and protecting the secrets of the glen from the world, Gaia needs to convince Levi to continue that protection. Daphnaie, the embodiment of his every dream, is sent to show him why, stealing his heart in the process to save her world.

Touched by the Sandman

A lonely woman's torrid sexual dreams and fantasy partner await her as a dominant reality in another dimension.

Dragons' Mate

Today Annie's dragons will shift and fulfill her every desire, which means a fiery threesome—and true love.

Keep reading for a sneak peek of Love Me Forever

Love Me Forever

By Beverly Ovalle

Chapter One

The road to Hell couldn't be any worse. Liam wiped the sweat out of his eyes, cursing his helmet, but knowing better than to take it off. He'd seen what happens when a bullet hit a helmet. He didn't think he'd ever forget. He'd much rather have that happen than having a bullet through his brain. He preferred his Stetson but that wasn't allowed in uniform and he'd stand out like a target if he wore it here.

Afghanistan reminded him a bit of the arid desert in Texas. Flat as far as the eye could see. The ground nothing but sand and pebbles, dry as the day was long. When it rained, the whole place quickly grew a cover of green, changing the bleakness to a sparkling jewel of hope. If you travelled far enough, you'd find the mountains. Liam figured joining the military would give him a chance to see the world. He didn't know the world he'd see would look just like home.

Liam wanted to join straight out of high school, but his father convinced him to stay for a couple more years. He took a few classes at the local community college but too many days of butting heads with his father over the ranch management, and Liam decided to follow his dream. The call of the Marines was too deeply ingrained in his soul to turn his back on it. His father should have understood. He had been in the service too, although unlike most of the men in the family, he had been in the Air Force. The men in his family came from a long line of Marines, it was in his blood to serve, no matter how his father argued against it.

Liam rode guard on the back of the supply truck. It was a dirty spot to be in, but they rotated so that everybody had a chance to eat dirt. He couldn't ask his men to do something he wouldn't do. He looked around, keeping an eye out for anything suspicious. Too many damn IED's found their way under the trucks. He had been taught the signs, but the damn terrorists kept upping the ante. Soon as they were able to start recognizing traps they'd change them again.

Nothing looked suspicious, but that just made him more paranoid. It had been too quiet lately. It was one of the reasons he was on lookout. This area had seen too much trouble. They passed the occasional traveler wrapped up in their burkas or dirty denims with keffiyeh's on their heads. You could see a mix of eastern and western influences everywhere. Not a big surprise as troops had been in the middle east for better than a dozen years.

They headed deeper into Helmand province, and the traffic got lighter. They were coming up to some hills, minor but a spot that an ambush could happen. Anytime you couldn't see the other side you'd have to scout. This spot in particular had seen its share of trouble. The tour that was here before them had lost three men in an IED blast. It was one of the spots they had to verify was safe before they crossed it.

Liam jumped down followed by Nelson. The outside duty was dirty, bad all the way around. It was their job to scout when anything suspicious was coming. In this case it was a 'been there, done that, not going back.'

They checked out the area ahead and found nothing suspicious. They turned, heading back to their position on the truck. Liam could feel the hair stand up on the back of his neck but nothing looked out of place. Waving the convoy forward, the Mine Resistant Ambush Protected vehicle in the lead headed out when the explosion hit. Liam and Nelson were thrown from the blast before they could reach the safety of their vehicle.

Liam heard yells and running feet and the crackle of flames as his world turned dark.

He woke up, his body aching, a thousand shards of glass grinding into his body. Trying to turn set up sharp spikes of agony until he once again slipped away.

Liam could hear a steady beep and the air around him was cool. The last thing he remembered was the dirt and heat that surrounded him as he went from FOB, Forward Operating Base, to FOB on the supply truck. He tried to lift his head and the steady ache had him setting it back down. Liam breathed deeply and tried to remember where he was at. Unable to guess, he slowly opened his eyes, squinting against the light.

He looked around as much as he could without moving his head. His eyes widened as he realized he was in the hospital. He recognized a couple of the doctors, so he knew he was still in Afghanistan. Liam closed his eyes against the throbbing pain and tried to remember what happened.

All he could remember was laughing and joking with his team. Then he woke up here. He shifted and bit back a scream of agony. Whatever happened he must've been right in the middle of it. Panting he lay back and tried to relax. If his memory didn't come back, someone would be sure to tell him what happened.

Liam knew they had been going on a run, delivering supplies from one FOB to another. He lay there, head throbbing and pain radiating up from both legs and his shoulders. Wiggling his fingers sent pain up his arms, his left thigh hot and burning. Any movement sent spikes of pain throughout his body. His chest was tight, stomach roiling, and he was afraid to look down. He didn't want to see if he was missing a limb. Liam had heard that even if you lost one you could still feel it. He swore he could wiggle his toes, could feel his leg. The pain and the cramping shooting down his calf. He didn't want to look, anxious at what he would find.

Eyes closed and denying what he knew was a good possibility, Liam listened to the world around him. Groans and constant beeping from machines filtered to his ears. Even through his closed lids he could tell it was daylight, the light shining through the delicate skin. He heard feet come close and reluctantly opened his eyes.

"How are we doing today, McGregor?" Liam could hear the scribbling of the doctor's pen as he made notations.

"Not sure, Doc."

"Explain. What aren't you sure about, Marine?"

Liam had to clear his throat. It was hard to talk through the dryness.

"I don't remember what happened." He turned his head toward the doc despite the ache in his neck. "How bad am I, Doc?"

"Besides the amnesia, which should only be temporary, you had a concussion." Liam realized that would be why he remembered being constantly woken up, feeling overwhelmed with pain only to drift off again. "You were hit with shrapnel from head to toe. You had evidently turned away from the blast point just before it went off. Your back was protected by your body armor. Your legs and arms took the brunt of the damage."

Liam needed to know at that point if his fears were realized. He swallowed heavily, his throat dry. The ache of tears he refused to release renewed the headache into a fierce pounding through his temples. Empty, his stomach was churning with sourness. He had to say it.

"I lost my legs?"

www.ingramcontent.com/pod-product-compliance
Lightning Source LLC
Chambersburg PA
CBHW061203170626
46809CB00003B/1226